I0549540

Wounded Birds

LYNN ALISON TROMBETTA

Published by:
Larksong Productions,
Earthsong, Inc.
Tempe, AZ
www.LynnTrombetta.com

This novella is a work of fiction. All the characters, places and events are either fictitious or are used fictitiously. Any resemblance to any one person, living or dead is purely coincidental.

Cover Design: Bob Haddad
Photo of Author: Rick Cyge
"Here Comes the Sun" lyrics by George Harrison
"Come Josephine in My Flying Machine"
lyrics by Alfred Bryan

First paperback Edition: January, 2017
ISBN-13: 978-0-9744878-0-9

In memory of my beautiful mother,
Charlotte Gail
and for the many women I have known who have each
pioneered their own unique ways of
surviving and thriving.

WOUNDED BIRDS

CHAPTERS

CHAPTERS

A NOTE FROM THE AUTHOR

Writing *Wounded Birds* was a crazy job, but somebody had to do it! A special thank-you to my Uncle Bob, who always reminds me that the solution to any problem lies within the problem. This thought was just one of many catalysts for the story.

Thank you to my dear husband, Rick Cyge and my friends and family who understand that once a story decides it must be told, there is no rest until it is done! You know who you are - I love you all.

-Lynn Alison Trombetta

WOUNDED BIRDS

1982
PHOENIX, ARIZONA

1 CARMELLA

MARICOPA COUNTY SHERIFF'S OFFICE, 4TH AVENUE JAIL

From within the darkened hallway, all that is visible of Carmella's small, frail body is the top of her head; her thinning, teased white hair crushed from her first night of sleeping on the meager pillow and mattress.

Mercifully, she is dreaming - her mind replaying the best of it to bury the worst of it.

Nick had turned her life upside down. When he sent a one-way ticket to Italy just weeks after the war ended in 1945, she was sure he was her destiny. They had met only once before at the VFW Post and although he was ten years her senior, it was love at first sight.

She would be reluctant to admit it now, but she still loves him…still dreams of him after all these years:

It is 1945. Carmella takes one last anticipatory glance back at her reflection in the luxurious full-length mirror. Swiveling her hips around, she notices a small wave in the line of her stocking, and pauses to straighten the silken seam. She has only seconds to smooth the front of her peplum and smile at the reflection of her 'finished self' before rushing to answer the door chime of the hotel suite.

"Nick!" She joyously presses into his arms.

"Let me look at you, Beautiful!" His hands are large on her tiny waist as he takes a step back to admire her. "Wow! Have I missed you!"

Nick lifts her off her feet and onto the posh bar, pushing his body between her knees. He smothers her lips with warm, persistent kisses as his suntanned hands inch past the top of her garter.

"Stop, Nick," she protests playfully. "You'll spoil the meaning of this special night; we have plans!"

He ends her sentence with a powerful kiss. "Shush, Baby. What could be more meaningful than me and you taking this all the way, right now?"

Carmella tugs at her hemline, "Nick, put me down! Let's go eat first. I want to see the night skyline and the stars over Italy, and drink champagne – all the things you promised when you sent for me."

Her eyes dart from Nick's beautiful smile - so close to hers - to his warm brown eyes. "I want to be dizzy and fall into your arms, like the first night we met…and we danced. That first night is all I've thought about for weeks."

Carmella's eyes sparkle like the stars above. "You can

have me then...I promise!"

Carmella stirs.

The clank of steel on steel somewhere nearby jerks her back into reality.

The thought of spending the rest of her life in prison returns, weighing heavy on her mind.

Carmella is the last person you would expect to find here. After all, she's had everything she could ever want. But she's also had a secret, and her greatest fear has always been that someone might discover it.

She tries to console herself: living with the secret for thirty-five of her sixty-nine years has certainly colored her life, but it has never, ever been more than she could bear.

She has survived.

Too bad she ended up harming others after all this time, this far down the road. There certainly is regret over that, but any remorse is certainly no match for her anger over the mistakes she made at the very end!

Carmella curls into a ball, tightening the thin gray blanket around herself. If only she had kept her wits about her. If only the others had minded their own business and left her to hers.

If only...

2 GRACE

CARMELLA MANOR, CENTRAL PHOENIX

"It is certainly more predictable than rain on the Arizona desert that nearly every day someone will knock on the door of Carmella Manor, the large yellow house in the historical district of Central Phoenix that I share with the other women. Yet you can hardly even call these visitors 'acquaintances' as the people of the neighborhood deliver wounded birds and orphaned creatures to me in shoeboxes and old birdcages. Whether it is a bird, a jackrabbit, a desert Javelina or even a snake, I'm never troubled by having yet another 'little soul' to care for, and I know I am most likely their only hope of survival.

While managing the grounds of Carmella Manor for nearly two decades, I've always felt good about the sacrifices I have made to care for so many animals along the way: I long ago realized that living my life this way is what I needed to feel worthy.

Yes, life should be about feeling good, and helping the birds and animals does just that! And that small voice inside me always adds, 'It pays something back for the fact that you lived through your birth, when years later your mother and baby sister did not: simple restitution for early survival.'

Still, a vague sadness washes through my heart as I play it all out in my mind and I end up feeling 'less than.'

'Less than' when compared to wealthy Carmella who doesn't even live at this beautiful home.

'Less than' when I look out across the decadent, manicured grounds of her estate.

And 'less than' knowing I might still be living in my tiny house trailer parked on the backlot of the San Diego Zoo if I hadn't ventured out and found work at Carmella Manor long ago.

But in my heart I know, I am much more than just the groundskeeper here. Here, where salmon-pink flowering Oleander bushes flank the property like ballerinas waiting to dance…where warm breezes playfully tease a chorus of crimson bougainvillea and a sprinkling of brilliant desert wildflowers as I walk along the flagstone leading to the pool.

And there, just beyond where the eye settles, tucked behind the grove of citrus trees is the large potting shed where I spend much of my free time with the wounded birds and animals that find their way to my care.

So I seek solace here, closing the door behind me.

Alone inside I escape the disapproving looks and demeaning comments the other women toss my way each time another orphan is delivered to the door of Carmella Manor. How dare they judge me instead of admire my efforts to save the wounded birds? At least I demonstrate that I care for something or someone other than only myself!

Just outside the window, my prize-winning Peace Rose glows in the morning light as a living testament to how Nature's beauty can be an antidote for pain and sadness.

I am reminded of poor widowed Aunt Mary who had taken me in after my mother and baby sister died in childbirth…it seemed a love of roses was nearly all that we ever truly had in common. She had tried her best to keep me happy, busy, and grounded in reality by dreaming up things for me to do. Why, in my teen years she had even tried to make *The Diary of Anne Frank* required reading. She did her best, but with the war and all, I was already filled with enough sad experiences to last a lifetime.

Can you smell that now? Smell the beautiful, nostalgic scent of the rose drifting in through the open window as the sun heats its perfume?

Thank God for the Rose!

You see, in spring of 1945, Aunt Mary drove us from Burbank to neighboring Pasadena so we could attend the first show ever of the Pacific Rose Society, where we were present for the debut of the Peace Rose! It was a fascinating experience for us both. The new rose, grown from propagated bud wood, had been shipped to the United States on one of the last airplanes out of France as World War II consumed everyone's thoughts.

When I close my eyes, I can recall every detail of the day that rose came into my life:

There was such a whirlwind of excitement at the show! Beautiful balloons and snow-white doves were released to celebrate not only the new rose, but also the impending fall of Berlin. The joyful display filled the clear, blue sky.

I released a balloon into the air, wishing with all of my heart that somehow I would know happiness. As I watched my hope travel up, up, up, twirling on gentle breezes, Aunt Mary approached carrying a small potted specimen of the glorious Peace Rose!

My heart leapt with joy... the same joy I still feel, propagation after propagation of the rose and its five-inch blossoms.

Sadly, that rose is now my only connection to the past and to any sense of family or belonging. I feel like such an outsider here. I had hoped for more from life; more from myself. But one glance around this workshed tells the truth of my life up until now: the Peace Rose, the wounded birds, and me.

There were times through the years I might have convinced myself to feel a much greater sense of being 'less than.' I could feel even worse about my housemates' obvious disapproval of my work for the animals and wounded birds ...except for the strong feeling that so often I am sure they look to me for not only guidance, but also at times even leadership.

In many ways, in my eyes they are 'wounded birds' too.

Especially in light of all that has happened this year..."

3 LAURIE AND IRENE

Laurie should have known the discussion of her memory problems wouldn't go anywhere with Irene, yet she has once again fallen into that familiar old trap as the women share their usual morning coffee. She tries to stand her ground.

"Irene, you always suck me into trusting you with my concerns! I know it's my own fault; you're not really a friend. Not really."

Irene does not argue the point. Using a slow sip from her coffee mug, she cleverly conceals what might be perceived as a smirk lurking in the corners of her mouth.

As is often the case, the worried look deep in Laurie's eyes betrays any outward appearance of calm.

Suddenly Laurie slaps the palm of her fragile hand angrily on the table to express her deep frustration.

"Irene, there is nothing you should find amusing about this! I mean it; we clearly are not friends! God knows I have tried, but the disappointing truth is that we just live together in this old house with the others and make the best of dealing with all of the baggage each of us ladies carries from a lifetime of trips to nowhere!"

Laurie's increasing stress over focusing her attention and remembering things spills over as she watches Irene walk across the kitchen to refill her cup.

"You're not the 'good little girl' you want people to think you are."

For Laurie, who tends to dress her own willowy-thin body in quiet beige and cream colors, Irene seems too short and stocky to successfully pull off wearing her usual primary-colored cotton capris, and she has said so on more than one occasion. The shorts happen to be red today. Topped off with a crisp white, puffy - sleeved blouse adorned with floral embroidery, the woman's color coordinated outfits seem more 'costume' than fashion statement.

Truth be told, ever since the women's California vacation together, Irene's nearly child-like garb reminds Laurie of the dancing Dutch dolls of the *It's a Small World* attraction at Disneyland. Irene fits the part perfectly; from the top of her yellow-blonde pageboy wig right down to her clunky, backless, wooden-soled clogs she appears as though she has just stepped out of the endless singing and dancing to the theme song at "The Happiest Place on Earth."

However, it is clear that Irene's not so happy.

"Try to get a grip on yourself, Laurie," she frowns.

As usual, Irene's tone of voice seems to have a particular shaming quality to it. Conversations with her have become increasingly one-sided as the women struggle to overlook her condescending attitude. That effort is so constant that it is easy for Laurie and the others to forget where the behavior springs from: how truly consumed Irene still is with talking about her recently deceased husband. It is as if her heart has frozen and now everything reminds her of her life with Barney. Yes, they forget...

And that, in a nutshell is Laurie's biggest problem. She forgets. And she forgets how often she ponders aloud, "Is forgetting the same as not remembering? If I've ever been able to answer that one for myself, I've either forgotten, or can't remember!"

Like the others, Laurie is no longer in the work force. Not that she wanted that phase of her life to be over. Sometimes change just pushes you along...ready or not. At the height of her career, she had been a promising young news reporter, truly a natural with language and writing. Now she finds herself losing confidence, and at times losing touch with the words needed for even the most basic communication.

Her discussion with Irene had begun innocently enough in the large sunlit kitchen of Carmella Manor. Over a reheated cup of coffee, Irene had seduced her into a false sense of trust:

"I just don't know where to go with this from here, Irene. Sometimes I remember, sometimes I don't. But there's always this feeling that I've forgotten something."

"Maybe you just need to quit trying so hard to remember and stop constantly believing that you've forgotten some small irrelevant detail."

"Really? That is like expecting someone who has lost her glasses to just look around and find them. If she can't see without the glasses, then there is certainly no hope of finding them."

Irene shakes her head, "Well, I'd give anything to forget how much I'm missing Barney, even if only for a few minutes."

"I should have known you would bring Barney into this."

"And why shouldn't I? Is there a difference between you thinking you might have forgotten something and my awareness of actually having a real person missing from my life? I am not able to forget that, not even for a moment."

"I do understand that. But when you switch the subject to Barney, I lose my own train of thought."

Laurie slows the pace of the conversation. "Irene, I can actually feel this happening to me. I used to make my living with words. Now I can't find them, can't always put them together easily, I'm frightened. I am hoping it is related to all the stress I've been under lately. Nevertheless, even if that is the case, that the stress is affecting my mind, I can't imagine how to get it all back. And like you, that awareness, that loss, never leaves me."

Irene offers no words of comfort, but for what seems like an eternity they gaze into each other's eyes, into each other's souls, until the doorbell rings and Irene rises from her chair to answer it.

"We can guess this will be another animal for

Grace," Irene comments, looking back over her shoulder.

Laurie follows close behind; a relic of childhood behavior in which she likes to see who's at the door, but is just too shy to be the one who answers it.

Irene does not attempt to be friendly when she opens the door. The stranger on the other side hands her a shoebox accompanied by a feeble 'thank you' and makes a hasty retreat before he can hear Irene grumble, "The last thing Grace needs is another mouth to feed."

Laurie observes, "The neighbors always leave quickly, as it seems they never want to wait for 'The Bird Lady' herself to receive the delivery."

"Bird Lady, indeed." Irene seems impatient, "As I've told you many times before, that's because Grace looks like some freakish medicine woman."

Irene begins to lift the corner of the shoebox lid, but Laurie quickly backs away, "Please keep it closed, I can't bear to look at whatever it is!"

Ignoring her protests, Irene peers inside. "Oh great. What a surprise; another pigeon...a rat with wings," she jeers.

Tucking the shoebox under her arm, she heads for the back door with Laurie allowing a few buffering steps between herself and the shoebox before following right behind as usual.

"Speaking of rats," Irene adds, "that crazy desert rat is out there barbecuing a rattlesnake as we speak!" She laughs, "I doubt anyone would ever come near this house if they realized the things that go on here. Come on, let's get this over with."

"Barbecuing a rattlesnake?" Laurie stops in her

tracks. "I can't bear to hear things like this! It makes me a nervous wreck!"

"Laurie, nearly everything makes you a nervous wreck these days. It can be somewhat entertaining, you know."

The sides of Irene's mouth curl into a teasing smile as she opens the door to the backyard. "No worries. Dead snakes can do no harm. And I've heard that barbecued rattlesnake tastes just like fried chicken."

4 THE MEDICINE WOMAN

The lawn has been recently mowed and the smell of Bermuda grass lingers in the growing heat of the day as Irene and Laurie cross the beautiful grounds. Grace, or as Irene calls her, the 'Medicine Woman' stands curled over the barbecue grill.

She looks nothing like what you'd expect from a woman in her fifties: Wearing a camouflage tank top and bib overalls with the pant cuffs rolled up to reveal colorful striped socks, her red bib apron sports three days' worth of soil from tending her flock. As usual, her dishwater blonde hair is tied back with a small, orange scarf and the short tendrils missed in the coif float about her head in unruly, breeze-teased wisps.

The roasting snake smells good enough, but you'd never catch either Irene or Laurie eating rattlesnake meat! The thought barely crosses their minds before

Grace grins and shoves a smoldering skewer toward them, offering a bite of what she obviously considers to be a delicacy.

A curl of smoky steam reaches out to entice Laurie. *Yes, it smells just like chicken!*

Grace's world is often beyond normal understanding; a curious mix of magical healing and a lot of hard work.

Laurie declines the crispy offering as Irene simply rolls her eyes and holds out the box, waiting while Grace takes time to enjoy a bite from the skewer before motioning for the pair to follow her into her animal workroom.

Neither of the women has been in the room for some time. It always smells of cedar rodent bedding, bird seed and stale aquarium water, so they tend to avoid the experience. Breaking form, Laurie lags several steps behind, pausing to decide if she will follow.

As Irene steps inside, Grace excitedly tells her the story of how she caught the rattlesnake earlier today in the chicken coop at the side of the workroom. She holds up a V-shaped stick she had used to pin the snake to the floor when she discovered it.

The last time Laurie visited, Grace had encouraged her to help gather some eggs from that very coop. It had been hot and humid that day and as the women entered the coop the chickens had startled; squawking and beating their wings wildly, filling the hot desert air with feathers and a choking, fine dust.

Laurie shudders with the memory: *And to think there might have been a rattlesnake in there for some time! It's puzzling that it has never been a problem before. Grace is entirely too fearless…and maybe even magical!*

Irene places the shoebox on a work table and Laurie finally enters, making her way past a hutch containing two jack rabbits, to the birdcage where Grace keeps the bright green and red parrot she calls "Echo." Laurie has a quiet fascination with this large, colorful bird.

"He's beautiful!" Laurie exclaims.

It seems the interest is mutual when Echo dances on his perch and squawks, "Boo tee full!"

Laurie giggles.

"Ha, Ha, Ha," Echo mimics loudly.

Grace gives a nod toward the bird, "THAT'S why we call him Echo. He makes sure everything you say to him comes right back at you!"

Echo tips his head to look sideways at Laurie as she cautiously moves in a little closer. The circular area of white surrounding his eye makes him look like a grease-painted clown, and, when he suddenly gives a loud "Squawk!" Laurie nearly knocks over his cage.

Grace dashes across the room to steady the cage until Echo's fluttering stops. While Echo preens his tail feathers back into place, Grace offers Laurie one of her homemade Honey Seed crackers to feed the bird. She gingerly pokes the treat through the cage bars.

Echo slowly, almost mechanically grasps the cracker and gently takes it from her, delicately nipping a surprisingly small piece from the edge with his powerful beak.

When Laurie brings her attention back to the room, the rear of Grace's grass-stained coveralls is pointing right at her. Grace digs around in her old refrigerator-freezer and offers the women their choice of a bottled beverage. With the animal smells and the general condition of the place, Laurie declines for both Irene and herself by quickly shaking her head.

Grace finally comes up for air holding a bottle of chocolate Yoo-hoo in one hand, and in the other a frozen mouse held upright by the tail, as if it were a popsicle.

Irene and Laurie recoil as Grace uses the mouse to gesture toward a small bright yellow snake in one of the aquariums nearby. "For the baby python," she explains. "I catch the mice and freeze 'em." She taps the frozen mouse against the workbench. Tap, tap, tap!

Echo makes a sharp, loud "Cluck! Cluck! Cluck!" to mimic the sound.

"It's my own kind of recycling." Grace laughs and glances sideways at Irene, "We'll let Mr. Mouse thaw a bit while we take a look here in the box at what the old cat dragged in."

"I could do without the 'old cat' metaphor," Irene frowns.

Grace moves the shoebox, placing it next to the stiff, frozen mouse and opens the lid to reveal a heat-stressed pigeon. She confidently checks the bird over and then administers some fluids with an injection just under the nearly featherless skin on the bird's back.

Laurie shudders with what she usually calls 'the willies,' but Grace just chuckles, "Give it a few days to recuperate and the bird will be just fine."

As she places the pigeon in one of the vacant cages containing fresh water and seed dispensers, her face glows with pride. She explains that although most of the animals and birds in her workroom are not sick, many would not have survived without her care.

"Yes, it's true...," her words trail off while she finishes setting up the cage and peers in at the pigeon.

Grace wipes her hands on her apron and sips her Yoo-hoo. It seems she is unaware she has left Laurie and Irene hanging with the expectation of hearing more about the animals. She snacks on a seed cracker topped off with the last of the rattlesnake meat, closing her eyes in bliss as she savors the morsel.

Laurie suddenly starts sneezing.

"Grace...it's filthy in here," Irene scolds, "Seriously, you need to clean it up!" Her shoes make clunking noises on the wooden floor as she wanders across the room and pauses in front of the aquarium containing three baby alligators.

"What on earth is the story here?" she asks, peering in through the glass.

"A man bought them for his three kids - one alligator for each of them," Grace chuckles. "Brilliant idea, huh? Then his wife learned she is expecting again, so it was either get another alligator or get rid of the three they had. My guess would be that bringing them to me was the mother's idea! I mean, what would they do with the alligators when they grew big enough to eat the children?" She laughs and shakes her head, "This kind of stuff happens all the time."

Overall, the room smells like one big hamster cage, but the alligators add their own peculiar swampy water odor that causes Irene to gag when she peers in over the top edge of the aquarium. A 'little one' stretches his neck up and opens his mouth to reveal his sharp baby alligator teeth. The tiny creature punctuates his threat by letting out a startling "HISSSSsss!"

Irene jumps backward and hits her head on the shelf above.

"Irene?" Grace laughs, "Why on earth, would you be putting your face within jumping range of an alligator's teeth?" She adds, "Just kidding. They can't jump. Those little baby creatures can't hurt you - unless you offer them a finger."

Rubbing the spot on her head and unsure of just how much to believe of what Grace is saying, Irene deflects the conversation toward making her original point about the overpowering smells and messiness of the workshed.

"Just look…why Laurie, you have a fuzzy pigeon feather stuck on your lip." She turns to Grace, "This is disgusting. Clean – it –up!"

"AWKKKK! CLEAN IT UP," Echo screeches.

Grace laughs and strikes a match on the table. She lights a small bundle of sage. "Clean it up? You know me better than that…I'm a lot like the pigeons: I don't do anything that requires too much effort. Why, do you know," she explains, "pigeons don't even migrate when it gets cold?"

The scent of sage curls into the room on smoky tendrils while Irene backs toward the door.

Grace continues, "Nope, as long as I keep the food coming, I'm sure they don't give a hoot or a coo about my housekeeping…or lack thereof!" She fans the sage into the room. "Who asked for your opinion anyway? God knows there's plenty to do besides housekeeping, both 'out there' and 'in here' just to keep it all going!"

Grace pinches the dead mouse to check if it has thawed yet.

While Laurie is preoccupied with attempts to

remove the last stubborn, wispy traces of the feather from her lip, she notices the Peace Rose blooming just outside the window. Her thoughts drift back to her very first assignment as a reporter for the newspaper:

Her interview with Grace about her award-winning State Fair entry of the Rose landed on the front page of the Gardening section. That's how they had met, and the article proved to be a catalyst for change in both of their lives.

Laurie had dreamed of being a writer for as long as she could remember, and she had done it! In days gone by, she was a well-known journalist with much to say and a varied audience who were interested in the thoughts and ideas she put down on paper. Now days she was just sure that no one was ever listening to what she was trying to communicate.

Irene huffs, "Grace, does Carmella know you have three stinking alligators in here?"

Without waiting for an answer, Irene grasps Laurie by the arm, "Come on, let's leave the Medicine Woman to her filthy menagerie."

Caught off guard and stumbling clumsily as Irene pulls her out of the workroom and across the lawn, Laurie has the uncomfortable feeling that Irene is only including her in her exit for drama.

When Grace calls after them, gesturing with her bottle of Yoo-hoo, saying she doesn't care if others make fun of her and that she doesn't see any of the rest of the women going out of their way to step up and help anyone...except themselves, something inside of Laurie feels Grace might be right.

5 ETTA

Leaving Grace's workroom and the animals behind, Irene holds Laurie's arm tightly, practically dragging her along until they climb the four wooden steps leading up to the back door of Carmella Manor. All the while, from the corner of her eye Laurie can see Grace's red apron flapping in the wind as she follows them toward the house.

When Irene turns the old doorknob, the door creeks and Etta begins scolding Laurie and Irene the moment they set foot in her kitchen. As Carmella Manor's longest tenant, Etta leaves nothing to fester when it comes to trying to get the control she wants.

"Oh, Irene," Laurie hesitates just inside, "we should have remembered how much Etta dislikes for us to enter from this back door, through her kitchen! If it wasn't for your dragging me along like some disobedient child, I might have remembered, but maybe not…"

Things only get worse when Grace follows them in, adorned with her dirty apron, and forgetting to wipe her feet on the mat.

Etta goes after Grace like an angry Chihuahua. She is a "little person" and she makes up for the difference in size between herself and Grace by shoving a stepstool close enough to allow her to get right in Grace's face.

Etta's body is round, and her short little legs stick out from beneath her clean white cotton apron to reveal sturdy black shoes with thin leather laces tied neatly in bows, reminiscent of the Pillsbury Dough Boy. She climbs upon the stepstool and leans toward Grace.

Her apron skirt tips backward like a ringing church bell, but the sounds that come out of Etta's mouth are anything but sweet.

She refers to the lot of them as 'pests' and in her most unusual voice, which is of a peculiar croaking, frog-like quality she demands they get out of her kitchen. "Especially you, Grace, you walking feather duster!"

Etta gestures grandly from her perch on the stool, "Grace, you're wasting your time out there with those deadbeat pigeons! Change your focus and raise birds to sell as food! Why, you could get sixteen dollars a pound if you could just clean up your act and raise the right kind of birds. Same with the frog legs, Doctor Do-Little! Hey, why don't we cook up some turtle soup?"

Grace leans in toward Etta's face, "Why are you always threatening to cook the poor creatures in my care? Do I have to point out that the only contact you ever have with the world of animals is with ones that are already dead and headed for a trip on your fork?"

Laurie giggles when Grace adds, "Food for thought, huh Etta?"

However, the glances from both women are not friendly and Laurie decides to make herself scarce.

6 THE ANTS

As Laurie sneaks away from the bickering, she notices the trail of ants she had discovered, and then forgotten a couple of days ago. Now, next to the table, instead of single file, the ants are traveling in a band leading straight into the pantry. "Oh yeah," she mutters, "the pantry where I left the pile of swept-up crumbs."

The women are still arguing. Laurie realizes she must stay and deal with what is clearly a growing problem. She tries in vain to get their attention to tell them about the ants, but it seems there is no stopping their rapidly intensifying discussion.

"Ladies! We must do something about the ants!"

Laurie runs to the living room and from the mantle of the fireplace grabs the first thing she can put her hands on. She lifts it high as she hurries back to the trail and prepares to smash the ants with several blows. She begs the women to hear her, "Please girls, you must pay attention to what I am trying to tell you!"

At first, no one is listening.

Then suddenly, it is as if time is standing still. Etta has stopped shaking her pudgy fists and yelling at Grace about her dirty clothing and the feathers caught in her hair and has turned her attention to Laurie.

Poised to deliver what is sure to be the first of many intended blows to a trail of ants traveling across the kitchen and into the pantry, Laurie is holding Etta's Golden Brick Award high above her head.

The treasured keepsake had come to Etta at a special ceremony many years after her participation in the movie, *The Wizard of Oz*. Moreover, since even Etta could not pick herself out in the sea of munchkin faces on the screen, the Golden Brick was proof that she had really done it.

"Oh no," Grace exclaims. "This isn't going to go well."

To make matters worse, it is obvious Laurie is having one of her anxiety attacks when she shrieks loudly, "Nobody's listening!"

Etta jumps down from the stepstool, landing squarely on both feet. Poised like a sumo wrestler, her apron flares out on each side of her body, revealing the checkered shorts hugging her ample buttocks.

Laurie stands momentarily motionless, suddenly the center of attention for Grace, Etta and Irene. "This is really important! Girls we have ants! We've had ants for days. We have a crisis here, and nobody's listening!"

"Calm down, Laurie." Grace reaches out to touch

her shoulder, but Laurie jerks away.

"I'm not calming down. I will not calm down as long as there are ants in this house! I'm not an outdoors-ey person."

The women notice a pleasure-filled sneer flicker across Irene's face as she teases, "Well obviously, these are indoors-ey ants, so I think we're good!"

Laurie seems to be trying desperately to survive the onslaught of Etta and Irene's challenge. "Very funny. I don't like ants. Girls, you should see how much garbage there is in there on the floor!"

Etta's eyes narrow, focused only on stopping Laurie from handling the brick, "Give me that – it's mine! What do you think you are doing with my Golden Brick Award?"

Clearly there is nothing Laurie can say to Etta to repair the insult, and she struggles like a goat in quicksand. The words come slowly, "It seemed logical, we have to protect ourselves."

Irene doesn't hold back. "Pro-tect ourselves? That's nearly laughable!"

Laurie's voice drops as her demeanor sinks a little deeper, "Yes, protect ourselves...from the ants."

"Laurie, do you realize how absurd you sound? Have you eaten anything today? You need to eat. Did you 'for-get' to eat lunch today?"

Laurie is crumbling right in front of their eyes.

"No! I haven't eaten, and I won't be eating. I can't eat...not with those ANTS! I've lost my appetite. You know how I am, I can't think straight with a thousand little stresses crawling around in our home."

Grace tries to reach out to her, to rescue her, but Laurie is still clutching the Golden Brick Award high in the air and it is clear Etta is not finished.

"It was you who swept the garbage into a neat little pile, and then forgot about it."

Laurie lowers the brick, as if she suddenly realizes how she is poised. "I left the pile there purposely because I wanted you girls to see how much garbage there was on the floor in there. We have to control this; we can't be so messy or the ants will come."

Etta lunges at Laurie, grabbing the Golden Brick from her hands. "Give it! How do you even have the nerve to think of using my Wizard of Oz Golden Brick Award to smash ants? How dare you?"

Laurie's eyes widen and are suddenly the bluest blue the women have ever seen. Laurie is not moving, and in fact, seems frozen in both mind and body.

"Wait!" Grace exclaims, "She's shutting down!"

As time seems to slow to a stop, Grace recalls, "Someone once explained why deer freeze in the headlights of an oncoming car. He had said, 'We wonder, stupid animal, why doesn't it just run away?' But it would be impossible for that to happen because a crucial part of the animal's brain simply shuts down when it is overstimulated…

Whether by headlights from an oncoming car, or simply too much stress, the game is over."

7 LAURIE

The last thing Laurie's eyes see is Etta lunging for the brick. The room has taken on a crisp brightness and in this very moment, Laurie does not have the sense that anything is wrong. In fact, she is feeling tremendous peace as the noise around her dissolves into gently twisting ribbons of color that float away toward a turquoise light in the distance.

Grace and Irene have stayed by her side, but Laurie remains unresponsive long enough for the ambulance to arrive. The sun-tanned paramedic kneels to attend to her.

"Laurie," he touches her shoulder, "I need to

shine a light into your eyes."

The light splashes into her awareness, and she can suddenly feel the warmth of his muscular hands through the medical gloves as he lays her arm across his knee. Laurie notices how the length of her arm terminates with her hand in his lap as he wraps the blood pressure cuff around her bicep. *Should I let my hand relax, it might touch him even more? Or should I curl it tighter into a fist?*

She watches his hazel eyes, fringed in thick, sun bleached lashes as he studies the readings on the meter and listens to her pulse with his stethoscope. For a moment, she forgets herself; forgets that she is no longer a young woman. When her actual age comes to mind, she realizes that accidentally touching his crotch with her hand means nothing to him.

Without noticing the intensity of her gaze the paramedic announces, "Eighty-seven over sixty-four. Have you been under any unusual stress lately?"

She manages the words, "Why don't you ask if I've been under any additional stress lately?"

Laurie wants to tell him how rapidly her mother's condition is deteriorating from Alzheimer's to worse, but before she can speak out loud, her thoughts run rampant:

I want to tell him everything; how the hospice wants me to give some directives for Mom in the event she stops breathing or has another stroke. I want to cry out about how unfair it is to burden me with these decisions. They wouldn't be asking so much of me if they realized my condition.

She decides to be brief. "I've been told I'm extra sensitive."

He smiles sweetly, "I can see that."

Even as she chooses to stay with the short, easy explanation of what the additional stress might be, it is in this moment she realizes this is the first time she has spoken the words;

"My mother is dying."

It is a good thing Laurie is already laying on the floor because she feels the shock waves as the words ring out, sounding as though someone else used a megaphone to announce the truth. The women are at once gathered round, looking down at her, and the view from where she lay makes her feel as though she has fallen into a hole…or maybe a grave.

My mother is dying.

8 How Do You See Yourself?

It is likely that what the paramedic is saying is not really soaking in for Laurie, but he is clearly wrapping things up to leave. He helps her to a chair and says he has written everything on the pink paper he sets on the table at her side. Etta hands her a glass of ice water and Grace strokes her hair.

The paramedic takes her hand in his hands to say goodbye, and there is the contrast of their skin…his so youthful, hers showing such age.

"Take care of yourself, ma'am," he says.

Her eyes follow as the women begin to escort him out of the room. She watches them go, and as the heel of his boot clears the doorway, her eyes pick up the trail of the ants again, forever marching it seems, sometimes three soldiers wide toward the pantry door.

Everything is primed for her: From where Laurie sits, she can see the "What's Bugging You?" magnet on the fridge and its bold red 800 phone number. The phone is within arm's reach. She makes her move:

"Listen, this is an emergency," she tells the exterminator's answering service. "We have a massive infestation of ants, and need someone to come right away. Please, it's an emergency!"

Etta and the others return just as Laurie finishes reciting their address. She chokes back the end of another repetition of the word 'emergency' when she sees them and hangs up the phone.

The women appear genuinely concerned over what just happened to her and seem to be treading lightly on how to speak to her. However, as usual, Irene tries to keep the controversy going with the topic of Laurie's intolerance for the ants:

"Laurie, are you still so consumed with the ant problem that you have actually taken it upon yourself to contact the exterminator, and call it an emergency? Dear, we are concerned about you, especially in light of what you've just gone through."

"Going through," Laurie corrects her. "The ants are adding to the stress I am GOING through. The ants don't belong in our home: I absolutely want them gone; g-o-n-e!"

"Little Pigeon," Grace advises, "you need to toughen up and quit thinking the world has to be perfect for you. It is all part of life. And we humans, and the birds, and even the ants are just struggling for existence, and no matter how hard we try, we can't control everything and make it all perfect."

Irene comments to no one in particular and as if Laurie is not even in the room, "Well, as usual, Laurie is unraveling like a ball of yarn over every little thing."

"I hate it when you talk about me as if I'm not here!" Laurie protests.

Grace apologizes for Irene, "She doesn't mean it. However, I have to caution that you can't always be seeing yourself as the weakest link in the chain and expect things to turn out right for you. We both know you weren't always like this. Remember, weak pigeons never have a nice day."

"That's exactly the point I was trying to make! Life really is a struggle, and we have to protect ourselves."

"But Laurie, you are missing my point. I'm not trying to say it is all a struggle – it is what it is: Life."

"Well, all I am sure of is that what it is for me is HARD!" Laurie challenges. "And it's getting harder all the time! I just want my brains back!"

Irene nearly cuts Laurie's sentence short, "Like I said before, you are unraveling, right before our eyes!"

Surprisingly, Etta comes to Laurie's rescue. Offering her the glass of ice water again, she frowns, "Everyone, I suggest we ease up on her a bit. Look, I do understand the fear that creeps in and weakens us…it's been a constant companion for me my whole life."

Her voice becomes gravelly, "Growing up in Germany, I was filled with fear. In fact, my future life had been in precarious balance as the war escalated. I'd heard rumors that the Nazi had a policy of exterminating 'undesirables.' And people with a physical impairment, such as 'midgets,' you know, 'little people' like me, were likely on the hit list."

"Oh, my God," Laurie takes the glass from her. "Etta, I've never thought about what your life as a midget must have been like during all of that turmoil."

"I have always hated that word, 'midget'! My parents said it was an old circus term, an artifact from days gone by to describe people who have dwarfism. When I later learned it came from a word that means 'very small fly,' I decided that circus pioneer, P.T. Barnum, who popularized the term, must have been the meanest man who ever lived! That is, until I got a little older and started thinking about Hitler."

"Gosh, I don't know how you survived it all!"

"We survived one day at a time, for sure. Mostly by not unraveling....extreme emotions like that could not be afforded. But I was being watched over. You could say that my physical liability became an asset."

"How so?"

"There was truly a miracle brewing in a place far away which offered me and other 'little people' an opportunity to escape our uncertain future in Nazi Germany. I learned that my height of only forty-six inches tall was just under the maximum allowed for a newly announced project with a German dance troupe. So, I joined... 'Lucky break in '38' I always say! They whisked us away to a California movie set just in time to begin filming on set for the Wizard of Oz."

"The whole story sounds amazing! How very brave of you," Laurie comments before taking a long drink from the glass. "I'm not sure I would have fared so well."

"Brave? I don't think so...I've never had much courage." Etta adds, "It was survival – do or die, I'm afraid."

Grace pulls a chair next to Laurie. With a certain softness she sometimes has, especially when she is tenderly hand-feeding a young cottontail rabbit or a baby bird she says, "Laurie, I'm listening to you talk. I wish I could help you understand how some of the anxiety you are having just might be self-inflicted. I'm just saying that how you see yourself - what you say to yourself every day is who you will be; and I think you are 'being' afraid. Afraid of life, and afraid of living."

Grace adds, "Why, I wouldn't even be in Arizona were it not for you! Laurie, you saw yourself differently when we first met...you were much stronger. What happened to that confident, intelligent woman? That feature article, the one you called 'Gardening for Peace' about my roses and me was a catalyst. You, a single white woman working with a staff of male reporters in the archaic 1940's and '50's...you aced it!"

"And if I hadn't saved that newspaper clipping...and called you at the newsroom so you could tell me about the groundskeeper position here; and had to you encourage me to travel across the desert to get it, why things would be very different for me, I'm sure! Come on Laurie, give it some thought. How do you see yourself now?"

"To my surprise, your words resonate with me. Hmm, how do I see myself?"

Grace waits for a response, but Laurie takes a long moment to think before answering. "I'd have to admit, I am afraid. I am afraid of ending up like Mom. I'm afraid of what is happening to her and how it relates to what might be happening to my own mind and me. And I almost constantly hear myself saying that I'm afraid of facing all of this alone. I want my mind back!"

Etta has her hands on her hips and has been eyeing Grace for the last couple of minutes. "With all the talk and free advice going on here, I'd like to know just how you see yourself, Grace." She adds, "I'm curious, especially in light of your messy work room and a wardrobe that rains feathers everywhere. Have you taken a step back to see what I see…to see what others see as a first impression of you?"

"In a word, I see myself as 'content' and as someone who cares enough about other living creatures to want to do things that make a difference."

"Well, it would make a huge difference to me personally if you would pay attention to some grooming and housekeeping details," Etta comments.

Graces dismisses Etta's opinions with a casual wave of her hand. "While you continue to peck at me, let me point out that with all of the chores required for tending things around here, I have more important details than housekeeping and clothing to think about. Besides, let's not forget: it was you who hired me. And speaking of first impressions, you offered up something pretty unusual that first day in the garden."

Etta shoots Grace a pleading look and waves her hands to get Grace to stop talking.

Grace laughs.

Laurie looks puzzled and Irene asks, "What's so funny?"

Grace laughs again, barely able to get the words going. "La-La-Laurie had told me about the groundskeeper position. The day I arrived at Carmella Manor, no one answered the door. While I waited, I heard the call of what sounded like an injured bird. When I, of course, followed the sound around to the back of the house, there was this pudgy little pink fairy waving a wand and loudly speaking to the blooms of two Oleander bushes and a Bird of Paradise plant. The fairy was so engrossed in casting her magic spell around the garden, that she didn't realize I was there until I tapped her shoulder. She jumped six inches off the ground, losing a curly-toed boot...I tell you, the last time I'd seen legs like that, they were curled up under Dorothy's house!"

"Grace! I didn't think that joke was funny at the time and I don't think it's funny now," Etta protests. "I was rehearsing for a job!"

Grace is still choking back laughter as she continues, "At first, I thought the fat little fairy was a child. But, but when I saw several rogue eyebrows growing from her chin, I realized she was not a child at all, but a much older little person."

"And that isn't funny either!"

"So, Grace, is that how you got the job," Irene asks, "by humiliating a fairy?"

"Well, truthfully, Laurie had already paved the way by telling Etta I was interested. The short story is that the fairy gestured with her wand toward the large building in the corner of the yard and told me to use it as needed, and that my first task was to check under every bush and clear out all the whiskey bottles left by the guy she had just fired!"

"Hmm, she was clearly desperate," Irene quips.

"Ok, you've had your fun." Etta commands, "All of you pests - out of my kitchen, hit the road!"

Grace laughs, "Of course, you must mean the

Yellow Brick Road!" To add to the annoyance, she opens her hand in front of Etta's face, revealing a palm full of feathers she has plucked from her clothes.

The doorbell rings, and as Grace skips away to answer it, tossing the feathers along the way, she teases, "Pigeons, and Gators, and Ants! Oh my! Pigeons, and Gators, and Ants! Oh my!"

9 GRACE, WHAT'S BUGGING YOU?

As usual, Grace is aware of Laurie's closeness as she follows right behind her to see who just rang the front doorbell. Before Grace or Irene can answer it, Etta's best friend flings the door wide and calls out, "It's me, Josephine, and a bug exterminator truck just pulled up too!"

Josephine, as colorful as a piñata and as loud as a mariachi band on Cinco de Mayo, bursts into the room with two armloads of shopping bags and several bright cotton totes.

Still drying her hands on a cup towel, Etta greets her long-time friend from across the room, "Jo!"

Grace watches Laurie tuck herself in behind Josephine to be sure to get a good close look at the bounty she has carried in, while a smiling Irene just tries to get out of the way of the commotion.

When Etta immediately busies herself with tidying up the room, Grace isn't sure Etta wants the company, but it is obvious Josephine is very happy to see both Etta and Irene. In fact, it seems to Grace that Josephine is usually happy and always seems glad to see them all, even though she can be extremely bossy if pressed.

The exterminator taps on the open door jamb, and Etta frowns as she pokes Laurie's arm, "Missy, did you get landlady Carmella's permission to call the exterminator?"

Before she can respond, Josephine jumps into the conversation, turning to touch Laurie's shoulder and reassure her not to worry about Carmella. "Etta, dear friend," she broadcasts into the room, "that old woman has enough money to exterminate all the bugs in this city if she wanted to!"

The Bug Woman standing in the still open door laughs, "I will make a note of that for future reference!" As the Bug Woman begins to laugh again at her own joke, Grace steps from behind the somewhat large stature of Josephine.

The husky sound of the Bug Woman's laughter catches in her throat at the sight of Grace. Their eyes meet. And although Josephine is rustling through her shopping bags, still chattering on about something while Irene and Laurie retrieve small boxes dropped on the floor and Etta announces how she hates it when Carmella 'gets her feathers ruffled,' for Grace the sounds grow distant and she can hear her own heartbeat in her ears.

Grace feels her face grow warm and a stirring she

has never experienced grows from deep within. Silently, she is overwhelmed. *Oh my God! She takes my breath away!*

Grace is afraid her demeanor will reveal her sudden, unexpected response! There is a magical magnetism between them, and as she tries to calm her runaway senses, Grace can tell The Bug Woman feels it too. Quickly she unties and removes the soiled red apron, rolling it and tossing it at Josephine's pile of totes. She edges the others out, nearly knocking Etta off balance as the women try to help gather Josephine's small packages.

"I'll handle this," she declares. "I'll tell her about the emergency we are dealing with."

Anything to be near her. Yet I almost cannot bear it.

Grace feels The Bug Woman's body close to her as they short cut through the grass. Head lowered as she walks; she watches her shoes and Bug Woman's work boots rhythmically splay the blades of green grass. When their arms brush together, her mind runs wild with the thought, *Is that tingling 'our' energy together?*

She had been too deep in thought to catch whatever The Bug Woman had just said, but now the woman is removing the grill from the crawl space between the house and the ground, kneeling on all fours to crawl inside. Grace realizes she has forgotten what the woman said her name is, and as she watches the back pockets of the Bug Woman's faded jeans disappear cautiously into the opening, she begins to 'see' herself acting this all out.

At once she realizes how foolish she must look, standing there watching a woman's rear disappear beneath the house and then lingering for so long after she has gone from view.

She stoops to look into the crawl space and calls after her, "I'm Grace. I'll be inside."

A few heartbeats later comes the reply, "Yep. I'm Amelia. I'll let you know what I find."

Glancing quickly toward each of the neighbor's homes, Grace hopes no one has seen her look like such a spinster - so foolish, so desperate. She makes her way back into her workshop and swiftly closes the door, trying to rid herself of the surge of energy she feels from being near Amelia.

I've always been on my own... I like it that way.

The Peace Rose glows outside the open window.

Before arriving at Carmella Manor, 'on her own' had meant living in a small camper trailer on the back lot of the San Diego Zoo working quietly as a groundskeeper throughout the day.

Grace's favorite part of the arrangement, aside from being able to hear all of the exotic bird calls from inside her tiny corner of the world, was the fact that the Zoo's administration had given her free reign over the gardens on the back lot and full use of the greenhouses. It was there she learned to propagate the Peace Rose, multiplying that one little stick of wood from Aunt Mary into dozens of offspring.

However, in her own personal life, she had never had the desire to reproduce, even when the Zoo's veterinarian was clearly interested. He had shown great patience, spending hours teaching her how to care for sick and injured animals needing to be isolated until their health returned. It had given them plenty to share, and many moments alone, but Grace had never felt even the smallest stirring for the man.

On her twenty-fifth birthday, Grace loaded up her Peace Roses and set her sights on the Arizona State Fair, where she hoped the plants would bloom in time for the gardening competition and tenth Anniversary Celebration of the war's end.

As she towed her house trailer from California to Arizona with peaceful stops along the way, the long stretches of empty desert spoke to her and she began to dream of living in Arizona someday.

10 JOSEPHINE

Josephine had been too involved with her shopping bags and colorful totes to notice that Grace and the Bug Woman were drawn to each other. Now that Grace has taken it upon herself to escort the Bug Woman back outside to look for the source of their ant problem, the attention has suddenly turned to Josephine and the shocking pink outfit she is wearing.

Etta's gaze momentarily sticks on the sight of her. She drops the small boxes she is gathering and squawks, "Jo, what the hell are you wearing?"

Josephine smiles, "I'm so pleased you have noticed even before I've had a chance to sit down!"

Bulging from all sides, she twirls round to show off her outfit, "They're my new polyester stretch pants for exercising!"

Irene simply shakes her head and retreats to the chair farthest from the discussion.

When Etta doesn't say anything, Josephine grows flustered. "What?" She lifts the edge of the matching zippered top to reveal the thick, rolled waistband, "They're sweat-wicking fabric. You know, sweat-wicking. I'm a sweaty…"

Etta cuts her off with an outstretched pudgy hand, "Please, say no more," she pleads.

Josephine's enthusiasm isn't fazed as she digs into one of the tote bags and produces a small, thick photo album. "Wait until you see this!"

Laurie moves a little closer, and when Jo notices her interest, she shows Laurie a few photos even before sharing the album with Etta.

"That's from a VFW party we danced for near the airbase when Etta and I first met," she explains. She leans in to whisper to Laurie, "Etta doesn't like to see the really old photos, especially the ones of us working odd 'character jobs' right after the war ended."

Josephine flips ahead several pages and calls out, "Look Etta, here are some shots of one of the mall gigs we did. That's you, in 1968 dressed as one of Santa's Elves. And look, there, check me out…"

Etta sits down on the couch, patting the cushion lightly so Josephine will sit next to her. Together they study the photo, "I don't see you, Jo."

When Josephine points to a specific area of the photo, Etta turns her head to look Jo straight in the eyes, obviously holding back the urge to laugh.

"Do you mean the reindeer's ass?"

"Yep. That's me!" she proudly exclaims as she slams the album shut and tosses it back into her tote bag without ever giving Irene a peek.

"Don't laugh, Etta. It may not have been my finest moment, but it was fun! We can't all claim our fame from something as grand as a 'walk-on' in The Wizard of Oz."

Etta retorts, "They don't call it a 'walk-on.' It was a Minor Character role."

Josephine stands up to emphasize the difference in their heights. "Minor...yes," Josephine adds with a playful smirk, just to even the score.

Etta tries again to change the subject. She begins to tell Josephine about the women's earlier discussion. However, Jo has returned to browsing the old photos and isn't paying much attention to the details of the conversation. She is surprised and seems a little offended when Etta asks, "So, Josephine, how do you see yourself?"

"How do I see myself? What kind of a question is that? Ok, I get it: you don't like the polyester pants! Too tight, I suppose. Maybe, too bright? Well, listen Etta, my friend; it is not as if I weigh 300 pounds! I'll have you know that the full length mirror on the back of the closet door works just fine for 'seeing myself!'"

Etta is quick to keep Josephine from further derailing her usual good nature; "Josephine, that's not what I meant at all," she croaks. "You are completely missing the point here! We girls have been talking. I am trying to find out what you think of your life: how you see yourself when it comes to your life and your choices up until now. Get it?"

"Oh..." Jo tips her head from side to side like a silly schoolgirl. "Oh, yes, I get it. Ok then; I see myself as happy."

Irene, seated in the chair across the room, doesn't hold back. "Really, is that true?" I know it's what you put out there, but is it true? I mean, aren't you kidding yourself with all the exercise classes and the jolly behavior?"

Jo's eyes flash with hurt and anger, "You're really nobody's friend, are you Irene! You know, you're not the only one with heartaches."

As if she is suddenly alone in the room, Josephine begins to hum a familiar tune. Soon the words break through and Josephine puts her arms out to glide around the furniture:

> "Come, Josephine, in my flying machine
> Going up, she goes, up she goes
> Balance yourself like a bird on a beam
> In the air she goes, there she goes
> Up, up, a little bit higher
> Oh my, the moon is on fire
> Come, Josephine, in my flying machine…"

When Jo stops gliding, tears glisten in her eyes. "My husband, Enrique always sang that song to me, every day until the day he died." She sighs.

"Look girls, to answer your question; I see myself as happy. I know I need to lose some weight, I know I live alone now, and I know I can be loud when I'm out in public. But the way I see it, this is what happens when you live alone for ten years - you get 'colorful' or you get sad. I'm colorful and happy. That's how I see it and that's what I tell myself every day. And that's how I survive."

11 IRENE

The tension of the discussion was not relieved by Josephine's gliding around the room to the sound of her own voice or by her declaration of her happiness.

Irene leaves the chair, and seems to be squaring up for another round, "I just can't believe you, Jo. I don't believe anyone is all that happy. I'm not. Not without my dear, sweet Barney."

Etta jumps in with full force, "I'm not defending Josephine's ideas about 'colorfulness' but I know where you are going with this, Irene. Do not romanticize your life with Barney. He was broken and sick for over fifteen of your years together."

The pitch of Etta's voice rises with anger, "Your doting kept him alive, but for what? So you could sacrifice a few more years to him?"

Etta is keeping just enough distance between herself and Irene to manage the difference in their heights. "You were sad and miserable. What did you say to yourself then?"

Irene looks down, fidgeting with the wedding band still on her finger.

Etta demands, "It's a real question, Irene. If you're going to make this about you and Barney once again, then answer the question."

Surprisingly, Irene seems to be giving in, just as she gave in to her life with Barney. "Fine! I told myself, each step of the way, that whatever was going on, no matter what it was, it would not last forever. That I could survive and keep going."

"See! Survival!" Laurie blurts out.

Etta responds with a hot sideways glance as she changes the tone of her voice, now low and grating, "And what do you say to yourself today, Irene?"

Irene hesitates and shakes her head, softly mumbling, "I don't know."

Etta presses on, "Well I do know. In fact, after all these years of listening to you talk about your life with Barney, and I mean the good stuff AND the bad stuff, I'd say I know you better than you know yourself!"

Irene is wordless, so Etta continues, "You say you miss him terribly, and every thought links back to him."

"Well, everything does link back to him. It hasn't been all that long, you know." Irene slumps onto the couch. "Some days are good, some days are not. I guess Laurie's right: it's 'survival.' Surviving the sadness; the loneliness; the loss."

Laurie tries to get a word in, but as usual, the

others pay little or no attention.

Etta marches on, "But when do you stop the charade? When do you face the truth about you and Barney? Nobody can do this for you, Irene! Because, as I see it, it's not the loss of him you are struggling with. I think you're struggling with the truth about why you sacrificed everything for the likes of him."

"Stop it!" Irene demands. Angry tears flood her eyes.

"Not until you admit that it wasn't all for love. No, you hated him. You doted on him out of guilt. Oy, I should know guilt when I see it!"

"I was good to him, right to the end," Irene sniffles as Laurie pushes a tissue box nearer to her. Etta's demeanor has become even more unyielding, "Guilt! Josephine, you were there; refresh Irene's memory…she told us all about it: She made a deal with God!"

"Irene, I don't mean to gang up on you, but there is some truth to what Etta is saying. I mean, it seems as though you've spent a lifetime trying to make up for having a little fun on the one night that Barney happened to have his accident."

"As I recall," Josephine continues, "When you and I met, you confessed that you weren't even sure you liked being Barney's wife! You often complained about living in that small apartment on the base. And you complained about the housework…"

"I wasn't having any fun. All I could think of is the disparity between being the sweet girl that Barney had proposed to and the girl who was on her knees close enough to the toilet to gag from the faint smell of male urine that I was scrubbing with too much Sani-Flush to get rid of."

"I had to laugh the day we met," Josephine recalls.

Irene first met Josephine way back when…she closes her eyes and tries to remember. That day at the laundromat must have been the first time they had spoken, even though she had seen her at the grocery supply near the base…

Josephine continues, "There you were; pin curls drying under a housewife's scarf, flipping through, of all possible things, the very well-worn pages of the laundromat's copy of *Good Housekeeping* magazine …meanwhile all the Ivory Snow laundry detergent you had dumped into the machine sudsed over and crept across the linoleum."

"Good thing you were there that day! In fact, good thing you were there in my life. You didn't even know me and you tried to mop up the mess with your own bed sheets!"

"I remember!"

"I loved how light-hearted you were, even as you slipped on the sudsy, wet sheets and fell backwards, feet into the air and landed on the seat of your pants! When you came up laughing, I realized a friendship with you might be just the medicine I needed to survive living at that air force base."

Irene's smile broadens. "I hope I wasn't too discouraging at the time, since you and Enrique were newly engaged, but I was bored out of my mind living Barney's regimented way of life."

"I could tell that's what was going on. I think maybe you took on too much, too soon."

Irene sighs, "I guess was so caught up in the idea of the engagement ring he placed on my finger that I missed the proverbial 'fine print' when I agreed."

"What fine print?" Etta asks.

"It's a figure of speech. I later realized I hadn't paid the greatest attention to what Barney was saying as he held up three fingers to outline his expectations for our union:

1. Good food
2. Good housekeeping
3. Good sex

'And not necessarily in that order,' he had added."

Irene pauses, then seems to be thinking aloud, "Ok, ok. I suppose some of it could have been guilt; I mean I could have, should have loved him better. I really wanted to feel that love in my heart. But he was un-loveable in his angry states." She swipes a tissue from the box and blows her nose with a most un-lady-like honking sound. "Especially when his injuries from the jet accident came back to haunt him later."

"Now we are getting somewhere," Etta replies.

"Getting somewhere? And you always say I'm the bitchy one? Just where is it you want to go with all of this? Barney had always been so strong, so authoritative…such a big, healthy, 'bear' of a man. The doctors said bone degeneration is what did him in. I watched his body shrink until he was just a whisper of the man he had been."

Laurie hands her another tissue. "I'm sorry for you, Irene."

"When he got sick and weak, I got the control! We were good then, and I grew to love him. But, I could not love him enough to make up for the lost years."

"But Irene, there's nothing to 'make-up' for: you were living with a corpse. It was a nightmare." Etta persists, "You could not love him enough? Really? Truth is you could not DO enough! And I mean that in the kindest way. You fed him; you lifted his bones from chair to bed, from bed to chair and back again. And when he crapped, you cleaned it up. Sorry to be so blunt, but after all, you were used to his shit even before he became ill."

Etta straightens her back. "Somebody tell me if I'm wrong here. Jo, am I wrong? Irene, how could you ever explain your level of dedication as anything but guilt? Guilt over years of hatred from dealing with the man he had been for the 'real' part of your marriage?"

"Stop it, stop it!" Laurie suddenly cries out, stomping her feet to punctuate the words. "You are being vicious!"

"No, wait Laurie, Etta's right…it was a nightmare."

Just when it seems Irene has sunk as deep into sadness as humanly possible, she adds, "Yes, it was a nightmare, I tried to make up for it, and we finally made sense…in his helplessness I could love him more."

"But Irene," Josephine comments, "you can't make up for something that wasn't your fault. Having a little fun at my wedding didn't make Barney's plane crash in the desert. You - we - had a good time. That's all. No guilt."

"I've always felt guilty because I was so excited and focused about going to your wedding and a chance for some excitement, that I didn't really listen to anything he was saying as he packed to go," Irene laments. "I just quickly kissed him, and didn't even watch him through the Venetian blinds like I usually did when he drove away. I wished he'd been able to celebrate with us, instead of flying off to California for something or other. So, yeah, when the phone call came about his crash, I felt guilt. And I made a deal with God. You would have too!"

Irene closes her eyes, not just to shut out the presence of the others, but also to try to remember something, anything good from her life with Barney. Yet all she could think of was that fateful day in 1945…

She had been feeling bored beyond belief with her life at the base and with Barney's rules, which he called "Standard Operating Procedures." She had settled into her daily tasks as his wife: keeping the small apartment tidy; keeping the hot meals coming at regular intervals for when he came in tired and hungry from training the novice pilots; and of course, keeping herself available to him for sex on a more regular basis than she would have preferred.

Irene could predict nearly every facet of her day, her week, and her month with near accuracy. She missed her family terribly. Were it not for her crazy friend Josephine, she was sure she could not bear her life on the base. Luckily, Josephine worked at the grocery supply near the base, so it was easy to stay in touch without bringing attention to the fact that she might be 'wasting time,' as Barney would likely see it.

When the war ended, Josephine and Enrique decided their wedding had to reflect not only the joy their new life was sure to bring, but also the country's elation over the end of the war. Enrique's family planned to drive up from Mexico to join other family in Arizona. Since a cousin was also training at the base, the wedding and reception would take place at the

VFW post. Irene was very excited by the invitation, and she spent long hours daydreaming about how she would wear her hair and what dress she would choose for the big day.

It was a celebration the likes of which Irene had only seen once on Cinco de Mayo her first year in Arizona. The joy was everywhere as she watched the little children dancing and listened to the Mariachis belt out their happiest songs.

The wedding champagne flowed and offered welcome relief from the chronic stress Irene lived with, and it was of some comfort to know that since Barney was away, she could enjoy a little freedom...even if she was still at the same base where she spent all of her days.

Enrique's cousin walked Irene home and as she fumbled with the keys, she could hear the telephone ringing inside the apartment.

"I'll be fine," she told her escort and she hurried inside to catch the call.

However, she was not fine; her knees buckled as the caller informed her that Barney's plane had gone down just before landing. The shock waves traveled from her brain all the way to the tips of her toes and her mind raced back to the moment she last saw him; the moment she had let slip by with her inattention.

"I promise," she had sobbed as she looked skyward and called out from her grief and her guilt, "God, if he survives, I will be the best wife I can be for him."

12 IT'S JUST WHO I AM

Laurie's earlier outburst had tempered the women's hurtful conversation. "Why were we talking about all this negative stuff from the past in the first place? Why would we do this to each other?"

Suddenly it seemed there was nothing more to say.

"It's time to end this discussion once and for all," Josephine declares. "Don't talk – just think! Nearly everyone carries around hurt and regret from the past." She has caught their attention.

"Look, I meant it when I said I see myself as 'Happy.' In fact, I believe the definition of 'sad' is to waste a lifetime on beliefs that just aren't true. I've had my turn at exactly that. So, girls, when does that end for each of you? I can honestly say that I am happy because I have chosen to be happy. When do you get to be happy?"

Before anyone can respond, Josephine singles each of them out, "Irene, when do you begin to live again? You have locked everyone out of your heart and you don't even know it! Don't you think that just maybe the fact that others are trying to tell you to lighten up and stop getting so worked up over the past, which you can never change, might be clues about the difference between how you see yourself and what you project to others? What you are projecting every day to all of us who live here with you?"

Not allowing time for a reply, she continues, "Etta, when will you have the courage to come to grips with the idea that life might actually be out of your personal control, and understand that that's okay? Laurie, when do you rise above your fears? When can you all really smile? For God's sake, when does the sun come out? Tell me, WHEN?"

"Now, enough!" Ever the court jester, Josephine decides to try to lighten things up by careening around in her polyester stretch pants, hips gyrating as she sings, "Here comes the sun, Here comes the sun, and I say. It's all right!"

"I'm in no mood for your levity," Laurie holds her head. "Please, Jo, you're making me dizzy!"

Josephine pauses in her steps and stops singing to ask, "Come on, when can you really smile? Just think about it, Laurie, WHEN?"

Etta adds, "I think I get it; maybe it is the fear of who we really are that squashes our happiness and has us running scared. I mean, like Grace always says,

'Weak pigeons are vulnerable - they're targets: They're dinner for something'!"

"The point is," Josephine continues, "I've made a commitment to look for joy everywhere, and to reach out to others in cheerfulness, even during those times when I have to fake it. Focus on the happy times!"

"Etta, didn't you have some truly happy times with your husband, Simon? With your having the courage to leave your homeland and living a past as vibrant as making The Wizard of OZ movie, you must still have great stories that even we girls haven't heard to draw happiness from."

"I do," she paused. "That's where I met Simon, during filming. You're right; thinking of that always makes me smile. But sometimes, it makes me sad too…I mean not being together forever, like I thought we would."

"Was he a 'little person' too?" Laurie asks.

"Yes. We were so lucky to find each other in this big old world. We explored every nook and cranny of that amazing movie set, and each other, I might add."

"Oh, too much detail," Laurie complains.

Etta laughs, "I guess we look at sex and life a little differently than 'big people.' Especially since life can be short for us. When the movie's costumer told me to cut back on snacks at the cast table between takes because I was getting a little pudgy, Simon and I realized I was pregnant. We decided to marry and found a cute little place in Culver City to stay close to the film industry for work."

"So you were able to have a child, just like that?" Irene asks, "I mean Barney and I never could."

71

"Evidently! Right? Simon had always teased me about my wide derriere - He would talk like a hillbilly and say my wide hips were perfect for birthing babies! And in spite of his diminutive stature, Simon was every bit the man – I mean size wasn't an issue there!"

"Thanks for sharing," Irene shakes her head, trying to hide a faint smile.

"It hadn't been a goal to have a baby. But having her really deepened the bond between Simon and me."

Laurie pauses, deep in a thought. "So, how did you end up in Arizona?"

"When the Japanese bombed Pearl Harbor I started feeling those old fears again and convinced Simon we should move further inland. His work at the studio had died down anyway. We found a little plot of land near Thunderbird Field No. 1, a United States Army training base in west Phoenix. We'd heard about the base when it was used for the making of the war film, 'Thunder Birds.' Remember that one, starring Preston Foster and Gene Tierney? Several famous actors - James Stewart, Cary Grant and Henry Fonda had helped finance the construction of the base and that idea made us feel as though we still had some tie, although remote, to Hollywood and the film industry."

"How on earth did you make a living here in those days?"

"We raised chickens and sold both the birds and the eggs for income." Etta's smile grows as she continues, "We were a novelty - the life of the party when we attended swing-dancing events at the nearby VFW post! Most evenings we enjoyed relaxing on the back cement porch behind our trailer, looking out across the undeveloped desert at the lavender hills in the far distance. And mornings, we watched our little red-haired girl playfully chase the chickens around the yard!"

"Aww," Laurie sighs, "was she a 'little' little girl?"

"No, in fact the doctors had been correct - the child was normal in size and in every way. By the time she was six years old we were all nearly the same size!" Etta laughs, "But, of course, that seemed perfectly normal to her. She loved that Simon and I could tell her stories from the Oz set about how we had met; and about of all of the other 'little people' we had known; and explain how 'The Horse of a Different Color' was tinted with lemon, cherry and grape flavored Jell-O for filming!"

"What did you name her?"

"That had been a big point of discussion for Simon and me, but I knew I wanted to name her after the film's main character. Simon argued that we were so much more than just the film we'd done together. And that was exactly my point: filming The Wizard of Oz changed me and changed my life. The experience meant more than I can say because it completely altered my thinking about how I felt about being a little person. That movie proved we can do everything that 'big people' can! And our own 'Dorothy Gale' is living proof to the world that this is true. We have her, as a normal-sized person to carry on!"

Irene seems lost in her thoughts as Josephine starts singing another chorus of "Here Comes the Sun" and twirls joyfully around the room. The Munchkin personality hiding inside of Etta surfaces to join the fun and she steps in place until Josephine passes by and then falls into line with Jo's gyrations, the large leading the small as they belt out more lyrics together.

"Here comes the sun, and I say; it's all right!"

Laurie's mind drifts back to the questions Jo had posed;

"When do you rise above your fears?"

"When can you really smile?"

Although she is not sure anyone is listening, Laurie says what she always says:

"This is just who I am! Everyone would see this about me if, instead of asking me 'WHEN' I can smile, they were asking me 'HOW.' Because, I haven't ever found a way."

13 It Wouldn't Be A Picnic Without The Ants!

It seems the women have finally put an end to all the discussion, and as Josephine runs out of lyrics for "Here Comes the Sun," Etta announces she is retreating to the kitchen to prepare a meal.

"The kitchen with the ANTS?" Laurie questions.

"Is there another kitchen in this house that I don't know about?"

Laurie watches Etta gather her ingredients. "I don't know if I can stomach food prepared in the vicinity of ants."

Grace has returned from escorting the Bug Woman around the property and as she closes the door behind herself, she leans back against it, as if she will swoon. Irene notices first, "Well?" she asks.

Etta stops what she is doing, carrots in one hand, and cabbage in the other. "What's with you?"

"Nothing, really. Amelia is checking under the house, in the crawl space. For ants."

Etta picks up her chef's knife and chops a carrot with lightning speed as she teases, "The Bug Woman? Oh, and now it's 'AMELIA?' Now THERE'S a horse of a different color!"

Josephine lets out a jolly laugh as she sets plates around the table. "Look at her, girls! Grace is clearly love-struck – OVER A WOMAN!"

Grace seems to be trying to control an overly broad smile, "She's a big woman, isn't she?"

"Big woman? She's a Bug Woman, Grace!" Etta's carrot chopping grows fiercer. "An Exterminator! What on earth are you thinking?"

Josephine laughs at the fun of it, "It looks like love at first bite to me!"

Irene interjects, "You could do better than to hook up with a BUG WOMAN. And besides, I am just positive it would not please Carmella to have a strange woman poking around her house! She's been a pillar of this community and having an exterminator's truck parked out front and a Bug Woman nosing around can't be good for her image."

"Her image?" Grace snaps out of the trance. "What about her motives? I mean I can't help but wonder about her. She is so absent and uninvolved! I've heard some harsh stuff about her through the years. From what's been said it would seem that old bird is a lot like a pigeon; I mean, she's far less famous for anything she's done than for the crap she's left behind!"

Everyone enjoys a good laugh, but Laurie notices a stray ant scouting the area beneath the table where she is sitting. Methodically, the ant travels in small circles, radiating outward, growing slightly wider as it looks for any morsel of food that might lead the way to news of a bigger feast to carry back to the nest and alert the others.

While Etta chops vegetables, Irene continues to offer opinions, and Grace daydreams about the "Bug Woman," Laurie watches the ant below her chair and drifts far away into a memory of her mother dressed in peach-colored gingham for a picnic by the lake. It is like watching home movies:

I remember...Mom unloads a bounty of chicken salad sandwiches, pickles, clusters of big, purple grapes and fresh homemade potato salad onto the picnic blanket for our little family to share.

On this special, sunny day together, Dad finishes his food and lies back, resting his head on Mom's lap. Her freshly pressed skirt drapes gracefully across the blanket and onto the green grass under the tree. Mom's face is serene while she lovingly strokes Dad's brow and the small stone in her wedding ring flashes brilliantly as it catches the sunlight.

At once, I have an odd sensation: it is as if I am not there; as if they are watching the boats on the lake without me.

And I am the only one to notice a single ant travel in zigzags across the gingham pattern of Mom's cotton skirt. I begin to worry the ant will reach Dad's hair.

Finally, I can bear it no more, but when I try to warn Mom about the ant, she quickly holds a finger to her lips, "Shhh!"

I feel small. No, I feel invisible.

But moments later, when Mom flicks the ant away - off her skirt, I am not sure what I feel.

Maybe, just alone.

As Josephine pulls out a chair to join Laurie at the table, Laurie's attention turns back to the ant, still circling below. Without uttering a word, Laurie quietly crushes it beneath her shoe.

14 ON THE TRAIL OF SOMETHING

The Bug Woman knocks and as Etta dries her hands on a cup towel and opens the door, she comments, "That didn't take long!"

Grace is all eyes and ears for Amelia as the woman explains she has found a large nest of ants near the back corner of the house.

"Right beneath MY room, no doubt!" Laurie comments.

"Not to worry," Amelia replies. "I can put some bait near there and that will be the end of them. But listen, I have to warn you ladies; It appears that the trail goes up into the attic so don't be alarmed when later, like maybe a few days from now, you'll have a whole bunch of ants pile up somewhere in the house as they die off and fall through the cracks in these tongue and groove ceiling boards."

"I can't believe my ears!" Laurie takes a step backwards.

"Try to keep it together," Irene cautions.

"Believe it, it's true. The ants will carry the bait into the colony, and when the poison takes effect it will cause the big 'die off' and there will be that pile of bodies somewhere in an unexpected place."

"Oh, my God!" Laurie pleads, "Isn't there some logical way you could think of to lure them outside, away from us?"

When the news sinks in, Etta frowns, "I'm not sure Carmella will appreciate a pile of dead ants in her house!"

"I'm not sure Carmella has any appreciation for *us* in her house!" Grace chimes in.

Laurie shudders and wraps her arms around her body. "Forget about Carmella! The thought of thousands of dead ants falling from the rafters unannounced is absolutely frightening – it is making my skin itch!"

"Well, and I hate to bring it up," Amelia chuckles, "but it will all happen again a week or so later!"

Jo is quick to interrupt before Laurie can react again. "Listen, we are trying to keep things calm and balanced here for Laurie, hoping to avoid calling the paramedics again for her. Bug Woman, you're not milking this for the drama, are you?"

"No, of course not, it is the honest-to-God truth." she replies.

"Of course it is," smiles Grace as she inches a little closer to her.

Josephine takes Laurie by the shoulders, "Listen, little lady! Think it through - dead ants are better than live ones! Nothing's perfect. It will be fine." Laurie shudders again.

"Yes," Irene adds in her sunniest voice, "and this time when you sweep up, you'll be all done!"

Jo continues, "And look; what Carmella doesn't know won't hurt her. Etta, just tell Carmella you are taking good care of the place by getting rid of the ants." In her bossiest voice she adds, "She can like it or lump it!"

Clearly not wanting to participate in the rising tension, Amelia has one hand on the doorknob, "Well, sounds like that's a 'Go-Ahead,' so I'll get to it." She escapes just as Irene pushes for more conflict:

"Stop being so disrespectful to Carmella," Irene demands. "She's done a lot in this community, so just quit. I mean it! She and I are good friends and she doesn't deserve this attitude from you girls!"

Grace waits until Amelia is out of earshot and then glides into the gossipy discussion, "Listen, Irene, from what I've learned, much of Carmella's charitable efforts go to help people who don't really need the assistance. "In fact," she jokes, "I've been told Carmella's ideas about what constitutes an act of charity are discomforting enough to make an ANT'S skin itch!"

"Oh, my God," Laurie sighs.

15 Baby Steps

Nearly half an hour passes while Amelia installs the ant bait and digs around with an old stick to check for termites under the house. Just as she is about to stop prodding, her stick catches the edge of what seems to be some kind of fabric, and with a slight tug she unearths the faded, water-stained ribbon edging of a small pale blue blanket, wrapped round with old burlap.

Extracting the bundle from the loamy earth beneath the home, Amelia discovers several artifacts from the life of a baby boy: a small glass and wood-framed photograph of a smiling, young child dressed all in blue and a little pair of shoes with tiny blue socks tucked inside.

"Thank God - no bones," she mutters as she loosely rewraps the items and makes her way back out through the opening of the crawl space.

Inside Carmella Manor the discussion has waned as the women share a hot pot of tea in the kitchen. Only occasional comments break the silence that has overtaken them. Grace blushes when Amelia reappears at the open kitchen door, catching her in the act of adding one last remark about Carmella.

Amelia offers up the odd-looking blanket and burlap-wrapped bundle. "Ladies, I found this stuff all wrapped up and slightly buried under the back corner of the house, beneath the steps."

She waits at the door until Irene comes forward and motions her inside. Laurie flanks Grace, as they all move in for a closer look.

"There was this photo of a little baby boy under the stairs! Guess you could call them 'Baby Steps," she jokes.

However, Amelia is the only one laughing as she loosens the wrap, and she seems caught off-guard by the way Laurie suddenly recoils at the sight of the photo.

"Oh no! Too creepy!" Laurie cries out as she backs away in horror.

The other women gather around while Jo examines one of the baby shoes. Laurie shudders, "I don't like this one bit! And you found it under the corner of the house where my room is?"

"Wait," Irene tries to slow things down, "this doesn't make any sense to me. Carmella is the original owner of this house - her husband had it built. And I believe we are the only others who have lived here. What do you think this means?"

Etta claps her small hands together, "It means we have a mystery at Carmella Manor!"

"Don't get all worked up, ladies," Josephine commands. "There's probably a logical explanation for it all. Just keep it calm and try not to upset each other."

"Good luck with THAT," Grace quips. "These pigeons aren't known for their independence."

Amelia catches her eye. "So, I just need a signature on the line, and I'll leave the mystery here with you."

Oh, those eyes! Grace signs on the line and quickly adds her private phone number next to her name. Amelia notices and gives her a little wink as she hands her a copy of the bill.

Grace watches her go, and then catches herself watching her go, realizing that Laurie has seen it all. She would have chastised herself for her desperate appearance, were it not for noticing the strangely dressed woman coming up the back walkway.

Etta notices too, "Now what?"

The woman's platform shoes click rhythmically against the flagstone. "Is Carmella Grant here?" she calls out.

As she draws near, Irene's fierce protectiveness for Carmella surfaces. "And who wants to know?"

"I'm Francesca...Frankie for short. I'm Carmella's daughter."

"Daughter?" Irene snaps, "She's never mentioned a daughter!"

Six thin hoop bracelets jangle as Frankie extends her hand to Irene, "Never mentioned me, huh? No surprise there! And who are you?"

Irene's stance hardens and she ignores the attempted friendly handshake. A wave of confusion washes over her face. "I'm her friend. That is, I thought I was her friend; until you showed up at the back door."

16 THE TEA PARTY THAT WASN'T

Irene has relaxed just enough about the stranger claiming to be Carmella's daughter to allow Etta to bring the woman into the kitchen for some tea. As Laurie and Etta arrange chairs and set another cup, Grace pauses on her way through the kitchen to feed the birds.

"Frankie," she queries, "If you're really Carmella's daughter, why is it we've never heard a word about you over all these years?"

Frankie slides her large duffle bag and a purse onto the floor near her chair as she sits. She lowers her head a bit, just enough to match her saddened voice.

"Because, me and her, we just don't get along."

"You don't get along? Really?" Irene demands, "That's it? I'm struggling with the same question as Grace, and the fact that you don't get along doesn't exactly explain how it could be that although I've been good friends with her for years, she's never even mentioned you."

Frankie is visibly angry, "That's so like her! I swear, nobody really knows her. She always seems all sweet and innocent, but it's just an act to cover up a pack of wicked lies and buried secrets. All I know of her is that she has left a trail of tears and broken hearts from New York to Arizona…and I'm one of her early stops along the way."

"Oh, no," Irene protests, "It couldn't be like all of that. She's my friend; we care about each other."

"Well, my guess is you think she cares - you think you are friends…like I thought she cared 'cause she's my mother."

Laurie nudges Grace, "Ask her about the stuff the Bug Woman found."

Grace nods, "Frankie, we have a bit of a mystery here. If it's alright we'd like to ask you a couple of questions about your mother and this house."

"Look, you're barking up the wrong tree. I left my mother's home when I was fourteen and never looked back. Her life is nothing but a big bunch of questions for me - her own daughter. You have questions?"

"Well, we just thought, maybe…"

"I have questions of my own. Why should it be any different for you? Listen, I'm not here to fix things. In fact I don't even really want to see her. Don't mention me to her, ever."

Frankie digs nervously in her large, over-stuffed purse. "Can I smoke?"

Etta stops dead in her tracks and answers Frankie in her most grating, angry voice, "Smoke? Absolutely not!"

The steam rising from the spout of the fresh pot of hot tea on the serving tray Etta is carrying looks as though it is coming from the nose on her reddening face.

"And if all you've just said is true, that you don't want to see her, then why are you here?"

"I was betting on the fact that she wouldn't be!"

Etta starts to pour the tea, but Frankie covers her cup with her hand, cigarette poked between two fingers, and hardens her gaze directly into Etta's eyes.

"I just need a place to land for a few days. Then, I'm outta here."

Etta's pouring of the tea becomes erratic, sloshing onto the table cloth as she shakes her head 'no' and tries desperately to signal the other women. A gaping pause develops in the flow of the conversation as Laurie tries to wipe up some of the spill.

Irene seems nervous and deflated, "Look, I suppose we've got to do something. Let her stay on the sun porch."

"Alright, Irene," Etta agrees, "but only to avoid getting you any more upset."

Frankie pushes away from the table, unlit cigarette and her lighter still in hand. "I hate to break up this happy little tea party before it even gets started, but I have to be somewhere else soon. Thanks for agreeing to help - I'll be back later this evening."

Irene watches her gather her things and go; her attention fixed on the empty doorway long after Frankie has gone. "Why didn't Carmella ever tell me about her daughter?" Soon, her eyes are brimming with tears. "I've believed we are good friends."

"I'm ever skeptical about Carmella. Maybe it's like Frankie said," Grace suggests. "Maybe she's playing her cards close to her chest and you don't know her well at all."

"I just can't believe it! First I loose Barney, and now this!" Irene turns her face skyward and bursts into tears.

Laurie hands her a tissue, offering what little support she can, "It seems you need to cry more than anything right now."

"Not that sob story again!" Etta snatches the teapot from the table, "What does Barney have to do with this?"

Laurie makes the connection, "Wait a minute, Etta. Irene...are you saying Barney's death months ago is the real reason you're so upset about Carmella now?"

Irene sniffles and nods as she looks at Laurie with her saddest eyes.

"Forget that!" Etta demands. "I'm just not buying that Barney's death and Carmella's deception have anything to do with each other!"

"Irene, aren't you feeling just a little relief about Barney," Laurie asks. "Since you don't have to take care of him every day anymore?"

Grace adds, "I was wondering the same thing. Aren't you feeling at least some sense of freedom after the burden of so many years of illness? You know, Irene, we've already covered this ground many times."

Irene hardens her gaze. "Relief? Freedom? Don't be cruel. I loved him and he was not a burden to me...even in the excruciating end. We never had children. I alone was there for him. Listen, I don't care to analyze it for you; in the end I truly loved him. No matter what! And sorry, but I can't help that I keep bringing it up. What gets to me is why don't I have someone like that in my life now, for me? Am I supposed to just fade on out gracefully - somehow? Without my husband, Barney? Now without my friend, Carmella? Without anyone watching over me?"

"You're not alone, Irene, you have us," Laurie tries to comfort her.

"Do I, Laurie? Look, I'm not trying to be mean, but will you even remember who I am this time next year?"

"That is mean! You know of my own personal fears over aging alone and Alzheimer's...especially with what is happening with my Mom."

"Me, me, me!" Etta's eyes darken with anger. "Irene, it's always all about you, isn't it?"

Grace interjects, "Look, some friendly advice here, Irene: Stop overwhelming yourself with the past. And stop harping on Laurie's memory issues. As far as Carmella goes, she's never even let you or anyone else into that locked room of hers downstairs. Maybe she does have something to hide. Maybe that locked room is a metaphor for her whole life. Maybe the whole house is! And maybe it has nothing to do with whether or not she is friends with you, or friends with any of us."

The idea catches Laurie's attention, "Grace, maybe that's what Frankie meant when she said that Carmella is covering up lies. Maybe that's just who she is."

Grace muses, "It does make some sense when you consider the way she cares about keeping up appearances, no matter the cost. That's something I've never liked about her. And this isn't the first time things just haven't added up where she's concerned. For example, the hit and run investigation, remember?"

Irene's tears stop instantly when she and Laurie notice Etta shoot Grace a look that warns, "Shut Up!"

"Hit and run?" Laurie looks puzzled, "No, Grace. I can't remember anything right now! I'm so confused. Oh, no! What if one of her lies is about that baby boy under the house?"

"Don't say it like that!" Irene scolds, "It's just a photo."

"That's what I meant...the photo of the baby boy!" Laurie nervously corrects herself, "That's what I meant!" She wrings her hands together as her anxiety escalates, "What if...oh God, what if someone is buried there?"

Grace grabs a small paper bag from the cupboard, blows air into it and hands it to Laurie. "Here, you know what to do...breathe into this."

"We do deserve to know the truth of the situation," Irene nervously reasons, "I could try to ask Carmella myself."

Grace pushes the bag up to Laurie's face. "Just get some control over yourselves, both of you! I promise we will get to the bottom of this. Laurie, breathe!"

"Grace," Laurie speaks into the bag, "I'm afraid this might be something even you can't fix."

"Shhhh! Breathe, and drink your tea."

17 GRACE, PLEASE WAKE UP!

Grace is dreaming she is traveling over rocky terrain, pushing aside bramble bushes that tear at her hands as she tries to find the source of the insistent plea ringing in her head, "Please, wake up. Grace, wake up!"

When she stirs and discovers Laurie's lipstick-less face and pale hair all askew in a ray of moonlight from the window, a moment of disorientation sends a shock wave through her senses.

"Grace, wake up. I remember where Carmella hid a key to her room!"

"That's amazing."

"Amazing? The key?" Laurie quizzes.

"No, the fact that you remembered something is what's amazing." Grace was just too muddled to resist the joke, which had been the first coherent thought to enter her mind.

"Don't make fun of me," Laurie protests. "Come on, there should be a little key on a short nail in the wall behind Carmella's husband's photo. We can use it to get in to her locked room and look for clues."

"Clues?" Grace tries to rub the sleep from her eyes. "Just what sort of clues do you think you might find there?"

"Clues about the little baby boy, and why his photo and baby shoes were buried under our home. And maybe even clues about her daughter, Frankie."

"Laurie, this could wait till morning."

"No, it can't! Irene will never go along with this."

"Not even after realizing her 'friend' Carmella has kept things from her?"

"No, I'm sure of it. Even though she is really hurt by all of this, she would still see this as betraying a friend. She will never go for this, and she'll forbid us from going in. It's all I can think about. Besides, I can't fall asleep."

"Well I WAS asleep!" Grace rolls over, turning her back on Laurie, longing for peaceful sleep without dreams.

"Please Grace, I'll never be able to rest and my heart is racing. You promised we would get to the bottom of this. Please!"

"Ok. I'm up. I'm up." Grace arranges her pajamas, untwisting the fabric that has wrapped around her leg.

"Aren't you going to put on some slippers? I mean, what if there are spiders in there after being closed up for so long?"

"Laurie, please! At least let me wake up a moment." Grace fumbles around in the dimly lit room before quietly slipping out the door.

As usual, Laurie follows Grace's lead, although tonight she is so close behind that Grace can feel Laurie's knee at the back of her own. "Geez, Laurie," she whispers, "Back off a little, I feel like a vaudeville act!"

The key is exactly where Laurie remembers.

"Good work, Laurie! I'm sure remembering this little detail means a lot to you."

Laurie huddles close, shining the flashlight she had remembered to bring as Grace quietly unlocks the door. The doorknob is stiff and the door gives a small moan and a bit of resistance at first. Then it is open: Open to reveal the room that neither of them has ever seen.

Antique leather chairs flank each corner of the spacious boudoir. A teacart with a full service of delicate china sits poised waiting for a chance of being used. The bed, which likely has not been slept in during all the years Grace has been at Carmella Manor, is richly dressed in a gold and olive green brocade bedspread with matching fringed throw pillows. There are tassels on the drapes, which are dramatically drawn back over a pull-down window shade that certainly blocks nearly all sunlight from ever entering the room. Large amber-colored globes hang from bronze chains on each side of the bed and when Grace flips on the light switch, the lamps cast a warm glow over the perfectly dressed room.

In fact, there is not a thing out of place. Grace and Laurie peek inside the bureau drawers, but stop short of actually going through the contents, which seem to consist only of neatly folded clothing, and in one case, fancy bras neatly cupped back upon themselves - more than any one person would normally own. Everything seems in order.

Laurie is admiring the tea set when Grace notices a sliver of morning light working its way in at the side of the window shade. "The sun is coming up. We'd better leave now."

Back in the comfort of her own bed, Grace had the urge to sleep late this morning, but she had trouble falling back asleep. Besides, the birds and animals need to be fed. She finally makes her way to the kitchen and serves herself a plate of the eggs and bacon Etta has cooked. Laurie is already waiting, eyeing her slow progress to join her at the breakfast table.

Grace is no sooner seated when Laurie leans forward and whispers, "Just because we didn't find anything last night doesn't mean it's not there, right? I mean that maybe we need to be more thorough. Let's look at this logically…"

Laurie sets the baby photo and the shoes in front of Grace.

"You and your logic! You're obsessing!" Grace tries to keep her voice as soft as possible to be sure Etta doesn't notice their discussion. "Dragging me around Carmella's room in the dead of night! We were thorough. There was nothing suspicious in that room. It's just a well-groomed room, just like the rest of

Carmella's perfect world." She pushes the photo and baby shoes aside, "I'm trying to eat my breakfast. Let's just drop it, okay?"

"What about the long crack by the mirror? That might be something."

"What long crack?" Grace is only mildly interested and as the other women prepare to join them, she is happy to drop the subject.

"It's barely six a.m.," Irene complains, "and you've all managed to wake me up." She pushes back the thin, unruly hair on her wigless head and scratches her belly in a most unladylike manner, "I didn't sleep well last night. I kept hearing things, I guess this whole thing with the Bug Woman's discovery and Carmella's supposed daughter lurking in the neighborhood has caused me some unrest."

As Irene and Etta fill coffee mugs and go about serving themselves, Laurie tries to take up where she left off. "The long crack by the mirror," she whispers. "Don't you think it's strange a 'perfect somebody' has a crack there in her room which she's never had repaired? It would give me the heebie-jeebies if it was in my bedroom."

Grace stares at the way the morning sun is illuminating the clear pitcher of fresh-squeezed orange juice across the table from her. Laurie whispers, "The key's back where it was. We could go in again."

Etta, carrying a plateful of eggs and a mug of coffee, scoots her chair out with her foot, "What are you two whispering about?"

"Laurie's probably imagining baby ghosts crawling around under the house now," Irene snipes. "That is, if she even remembers what the Bug Woman found under there."

Laurie groups the photo and baby shoes together, "Did you all stop to think, these could be clues to something serious?"

Grace has had enough, "Alright! As far as this mystery thing goes, it has been my experience that circumstances do not create a man, they reveal him. I'd say whatever this is all about, whatever's being revealed here, is just a product of the way that 'perfect,' perfectly selfish woman Carmella has lived her whole life. Look Laurie, I have chores to do. We all have things to do."

She stacks her dishes and stands to leave, but sits back into her chair when Irene announces, "Carmella's coming over. I called her about Frankie."

"Are you crazy?" Etta scolds, "I heard you promise Frankie you wouldn't tell Carmella that her daughter has turned up."

"I have my loyalties," Irene declares.

"Yes, I see that." Etta croaks, "Yep, I can see all about your loyalties. I see that even after realizing that the woman has not been truthful with you, you're still loyal. Hmmm..."

Grace takes the photo and baby shoes from Laurie and studies the boy's face, while Etta continues, "Carmella's deceit would have put a serious crack in my friendship with her."

Grace thinks aloud, softly, "Okay...so maybe that is it. The Crack. The crack in the wall, the flaw in the perfection!"

"What?" Laurie had heard Grace mutter.

"Nothing," she replies, as she heads for the door.

18 THE EYE OF THE TORNADO

The walk out to the workshed provides Grace some welcome separation from the other women. Opening the door, she smiles as she looks around at the messiness. Keeping the place dirty like this might actually be some form of defense for keeping the others away, even though all she has ever wanted from them was a sense of belonging…a feeling she has never known at Carmella Manor.

She goes about her chores, spending a little time with each of the birds, checking the cast on the jackrabbit's broken leg, and throwing some fresh ground beef in with the baby alligators. She even talks to the turtle, which she happily notes is beginning to respond to her voice and the shaking of a turtle food can when she feeds him each day.

Grace keeps busy all morning while batches of her recipe for Honey Seed crackers bake in the oven, and when each batch has cooled, she restocks all of the Tupperware containers with the crackers and stacks them neatly on the bottom shelves near the birds.

After covering the stored containers with a colorful Indian blanket, she cuts the very last batch for herself and fills a couple of small bags with the crackers to snack on later. Tucking them into her apron pouch, she has all but forgotten about the non-productive excursion into Carmella's room with Laurie in the wee hours of the night. That is, until she dozes off in the sun warming the wicker chair next to Echo's cage...

Suddenly Grace's sleeping mind is whirling with the memory of artifacts from Carmella's perfect room: everything is spinning and moving in circles - as though she is caught at the center of a tornado. The fancy leather chairs, Carmella's lacy bras and the gold-tasseled throw pillows are wildly flying about.

In the dream, an Oriental rug she is standing on suddenly lurches away from the floor, forcing her to sit, and with a "Bang!" the window shade rolls up and the rug transports Grace away, out through the open window. Away over rooftops, over cities. Away, high into the night sky, bringing her down to rest on the veranda of a villa. She can hear voices speaking in what seems to be Italian, although she is unable to understand anything of the distant words.

There, in the courtyard just below is a couple dancing. They have slowed, off-beat for the muffled music floating across from somewhere nearby. The air is sweet with fragrant flowers and the sky is brimming with stars. The man touches the woman's face and gently kisses her lips. She has clearly surrendered to him, and they hold each other as if the world will end in the next moment.

Suddenly, the dream is shattered and everything falls apart. The carpet flips up and away and Grace feels herself falling backward; falling and falling! A loud screeching sound pierces the air, culminating in a large 'Crash!'

Grace opens her eyes. Echo's cage is sideways on the floor and his feathers are soaking wet as he tips his head and peers out at her, pacing back and forth over the cage bars that now rest on the floor.

The wicker chair and Grace are covered in sunflower seed shells and dried bird poop. As Grace picks herself up and dusts the debris from her apron, she realizes she had been so tired that she dozed off with her feet up, precariously tipped back in the wicker chair. At some point, the whole situation had just fallen apart as Grace lost her balance!

Grace checks the pouch of her apron. Somehow, the newly baked Honey Seed crackers have escaped being crushed. However, as she looks over the mess and everything that has scattered, she begins to recall ever more details from the dream that had taken her away to what seemed like another time and to a place she had never experienced before. She remembers the flying lace bras and swirling leather chairs.

Suddenly she knows it: she has to go back. It is as if something in Carmella's room is calling her to return.

The others have busied themselves elsewhere, and as soon as Grace is reasonably sure she will not be noticed, she hooks a small flashlight on her belt and sneaks through the halls, wary of anyone who might see her there. Lifting the edge of the photo of Carmella's husband, she retrieves the key. As she quietly unlocks the door and replaces the key, lowering the photo back into position, she truly notices his eyes, which seem to be staring directly into hers.

Quickly, into the room…she shuts the door behind her! Locating the crack that Laurie had mentioned is easy. She wonders how she didn't notice it before: a quarter-inch wide, craggy opening extending from the edge of the massive mirror down into the place where the plaster wall meets the wooden floor. It is indeed strange that Carmella has never had it repaired.

Intuitively, Grace lifts the Oriental rug and discovers a round wooden plug, and underneath, a small lever, inset into the floor. When she barely touches the lever, the mirror swings wide with a strange moan, knocking her backward onto her heels. A secret passage and stairs extending down into darkness is revealed.

Nearly fearless and never one to shy away from a challenge, Grace unhooks the flashlight from her belt and peers inside. Slowly, carefully, she makes her way, one curious step at a time, into the heart of a mystery.

19 Meanwhile, In Another Part Of The House...

Carmella arrives in a huff to find Irene, still in her robe, seated on the couch quietly reading a magazine.

"Oh good, Carmella...I'm so relieved to see you." Irene rushes toward the perfectly dressed woman to greet her, but Carmella clearly is not pleased and twists away. Turning her back on Irene, she tosses the satchel she is carrying onto a chair.

"Irene, where's Frankie! Where is she?"

"She never came back last night. Carmella, why haven't you ever told me about her?" Irene doesn't try to conceal the hurt she feels.

"Why should I, Irene? I hadn't expected to be dealing with this from you. How is it your business? If you must know, I haven't seen her in years."

"It's not that I 'must know,' it's that you and I are friends - we share things."

"Friends? Oh, Irene, it's way too early in the morning for all of this. Friendly and friendship are two different things. Where ever did you get the idea that it is more than it is?"

"Carmella, please, we've known each other for years. I've thought of you as my friend all along. My God, you have a real, living daughter you've never mentioned. She's all grown up!"

"Irene, I certainly don't owe you any explanation. Especially about Frankie! That little streetwalker is something I'd just rather forget. Let me know if she shows up. I'll be in my room for now, but I'm not staying - I have a hotel room in town."

Carmella retrieves the satchel and with quick, angry steps, she storms down the long hallway to her room.

As she begins to unlock the door to her very private space, it opens without resistance, as if it is not locked at all. Carmella glances into the room.

There! The mirror is turned back on its massive hinges, and the stairwell is revealed. She closes the door and tiptoes in, being careful to avoid the one squeaky floor board which she knows will surely creek under her weight. Staring in to the darkness from the side of the opening she waits for her eyesight to adjust.

In the muted light below, the roving beam of a flashlight affords the briefest glimpse of Grace's red apron. "Oh, no..." she whispers to herself.

Before Carmella can even think about what she 'should' do, she pushes the teacart straight into the opening, teacups and all. There is the sound of the cart falling, falling, falling, end over end, stair-by-stair, porcelain tea cups breaking rhythmically as they crash to the ground and shatter against each other at each turn of the cart. Without waiting for the falling to end, and for the cart to hit bottom, Carmella quickly slams the mirror passage shut and locks the lever back into place.

Like a small child who has just created a mess, Carmella pauses, her fingertips pressed to her lips, as if trying to decide what to do next.

With one short, final glance around the room Carmella stashes the satchel behind the headboard of her bed. Then…checking the empty hallway, she backs out the doorway and locks the door behind her.

In the darkness below, Grace moans. *Was that Carmella at the top of the stairwell?*

As she begins to comprehend only some of what has happened to her, her first thoughts are not on the pain she feels in her arm and shoulder, but on the animals she cares for. *Crap! Who's going to feed the birds?*

Alone, unable to move, and unsure of how much time has passed, Grace can only watch as the flashlight illuminating the dirt cellar floor grows dim and dies.

20 SCREW THE DAMNED BIRDS!

Pale light spilling in from a small screened opening too high to reach is Grace's only clue that an entire night has passed. A pigeon returns to its nest there, just outside on the ledge.

Propping herself up against the cellar wall, Grace is suffering a lot of pain caused by her fall when the teacart met her halfway up the stair well.

She talks to the pigeon, hoping the conversation will lead her to a plan for getting out of her predicament. "This is a switch: You're free, I'm not. Too bad you're not a trained carrier pigeon so I could get a message out."

The pigeon wriggles and settles down onto the tangled nest answering with only the softest of a cooing noise.

Grace's thoughts run rampant and she speaks aloud. "Damn it! I haven't heard the others even call my name! It's as if I never existed! As if I was never here! What if I die here, in this musty old cellar?"

The pigeon is quiet as Grace continues.

"I stowed nearly all of all the Honey Seed crackers and have the rest with me – the others won't know where to look for what to feed the birds. That's if they even think of it at all. And if the girls upstairs are not thinking about me, then they're certainly not thinking about my birds. That means the birds are going to starve to death!"

Grace tries to get more comfortable but realizes her injuries may be worse than she had thought at first. The fear that all of this could end her life suddenly grips her imagination.

She calls up to the pigeon, "I certainly never pictured it like this...my death, I mean. Alone in a dirt-floored basement. Okay, alone, yes. I admit it, But alone in a basement? No!' My head is pounding, and I'm so thirsty. What the Hell!"

She can see the pigeon tip its head to look down at her with one eye. "Birdy, we can take a lesson from this, you know? Crap! This is why you truly can't be dependent on others in any way!" She struggles to shift her position.

"Hey, stupid pigeon! Are you listening? I said; you can't be dependent on others. Nobody is coming to the rescue! I mean it! It's just not true that someone will always be there, sitting on a park bench waiting to feed you breadcrumbs! It's an unpleasant fact! There are far too many pigeons and far too few kind-hearted people with time and concern for the likes of you and me!"

Grace rubs her aching shoulder. "Got that? And that's not even the worst of it: I learned the hard way that if you believe for one moment that everyone who offers to help you, to feed you, is doing it out of kindness, well then you're headed for a squab dinner, my friend."

The pigeon makes quiet cooing sounds and fluffs her feathers as the sweet smell of creosote signals the coming of rain on the desert. Safe upon her nest in the little alcove, the bird seems undisturbed by Grace's tirade or the downpour that soon follows.

The thunderstorm offers a strange degree of comfort and Grace gives in to sleep at the pervasive, rhythmic sound of the falling rain.

In her slumber, Grace dreams of spiders. Thousands, upon thousands of spiders. She is startled awake when something touches her hand, only to discover that a small stream of rainwater now glides down the bricks next to her, enough to puddle at her fingertips resting on the dirt. Grace turns slightly to sip the fresh water flowing down the wall and rests her cheek against the coolness.

She closes her eyes again. The spiders are replaced by thoughts of all of the many people she has helped over the years. People whom, for the most part never returned her favors when she needed assistance along the way.

She tries not to think dark thoughts, but it seems she has nearly always had to fend for herself. There were so many times she had to be strong when she really needed someone else to help. "And here I am....alone again."

Grace begins to panic from the dankness and she calls out in the dim light, "Pigeon? I don't want to die here!" The bird does not stir. Anger and fear squeeze out from Grace's clenched teeth, "Screw you, pigeon! In fact, screw all the damn birds! My God! What have I done with my life? I gave it all away. It can't end like this!"

Suddenly releasing a flood of tears, Grace curls against the wall. "Aw, Mom, I'm so sorry!"

She looks up at the opening where daylight silhouettes the pigeon, "I was just a kid. How could I know you were dying? I didn't even know the baby had been born! Why did she die too?"

Grace struggles to her feet, seeking the comfort of a little more sunlight. "Pigeon, I swear I have tried to make it up to her - I've tried to fix so many wounded birds and broken animals, anywhere I could, more souls than could ever be counted! I just need to fix things, to make it right. For Mom ... and for the baby."

Her anger quiets into softly flowing tears, "Mom, if you can hear me, let me know somehow... I was good. Let me know I haven't wasted my life. Mom, please!"

Grace moves slowly along the wall. Her foot catches on something in the dark, sending her tumbling to the earthen floor.

She glides her hand across the dirt to find what has caused her to fall. Her fingers close around a cold hard object. She easily pulls it loose from the earth and lifts the lightweight length of it into the dim light from the opening where the bird sits. Her eyes try to adjust.

"Shit!" She recoils, instantly releasing the object. "A leg bone!"

Grace scoots backward in the dirt and tries to catch her breath. Her heart feels as if it will leap from her chest. "Somebody's femur!" Slowly, she catches her breath. "Well I'll be dammed."

The sky outside darkens and it begins to rain again.

Somehow, Grace finds unexpected humor in her discovery and exhales a chuckle, "It looks like Frankie was telling the truth: evidently Carmella really does bury her secrets!"

21 LAURIE: "IT LOOKS LIKE I'M ON MY OWN"

Laurie is pacing and wringing her hands. Etta and Irene are seated for breakfast at the table.

"Please, Laurie. We are trying very hard to avoid getting sucked into your drama."

"But, I'm worried sick! It's been almost two days since we've seen Grace. She didn't say she was going anywhere."

"And you would remember if she did?" Etta questions.

"Well, I think I would."

Irene does not miss a beat, "Laurie," she taunts, "It's just as likely Grace DID tell you where she was going and you've forgotten. You'd forget your own name if we weren't here to remind you. Let's try not to worry."

"I can't help but worry. I can only think of poor Grace, and what if she's hurt somewhere?"

"So that's what's been going around and around in that obsessive little brain of yours? You let your imagination run wild and now you think she is hurt?"

It seems Laurie can barely control her temper, "Don't act surprised! You just haven't been listening. No one listens to me anymore. No one takes me seriously. It's bad enough that Grace is missing, but no one will hear me about this. I'm giving up on trying with you girls!" She puts her hands on her waist and defiantly declares, "I called the police, you know."

Irene nearly drops her cup and saucer, "The police? Oh, come on now. Really?"

"I did. I told them that Grace is missing and that Frankie never came back. Maybe there's a kidnapper in the neighborhood. It's a logical possibility."

Etta looks concerned, "Oh, Laurie, You shouldn't have involved them. Carmella's due back any time now and we cannot have a squad of police cars out in front of the house when she arrives. She's angry enough already!"

Laurie throws up her hands in despair, "Don't worry, they barely listened to me - same as everyone else here...the police won't come until Grace has been gone for more than forty-eight hours. It's a stupid rule. What if she's in trouble? What if she needs us?"

"Well," Etta offers, "If someone needs us, it surely isn't Grace." She picks up a stack of folded towels, "Grace will show up. Stop fretting."

Laurie waits for Etta to leave the room before turning to whisper softly to Irene, "Irene, let's go look in Carmella's room. I once saw where she hides the key. Maybe there are clues there inside."

Irene slams her coffee mug onto the table, "Absolutely not! Whatever makes you think Carmella's room would have anything to do with this?"

Laurie is startled but decides to go ahead, "I didn't want to tell you, but Grace and I went in there the night before Grace disappeared. I just thought with Carmella always being so secretive, even about her daughter, Frankie; well, just maybe..."

The phone offers an untimely interruption, but before answering it Irene replies in no uncertain terms, "No! We are not going into her room. I'm sure she's locked it for a reason. No! Not on your life!"

By Irene's responses, clearly it is Frankie on the phone, apologizing for not calling to let Irene know she was not coming back the night she arrived. When the call ends, Irene dials another number without any hesitation. "Carmella, I just heard from Frankie...she's on her way back here."

Clearly, Irene's loyalty to Carmella has no limit.

There is no way Laurie will rest until she checks Carmella's room one more time for any clues that might help find Grace. Her mind is reeling. In spite of knowing that Irene thinks it is wrong and Etta thinks she is crazy for even imagining something has happened to Grace, Laurie is sure Grace would never leave without saying where she was going.

It had been pouring rain this morning as she made her way across the water soaked lawn to Grace's workshed, so she couldn't help but worry even more about her safety. She had done what she could to feed some of the animals…but she could not find where Grace keeps the Honey Seed crackers and some of the other animal food, and certainly was unsure of how and what she should feed the alligators.

"This is all too frustrating, Echo" she had told the parrot. "I don't know where anything is for the animals, and I still don't' know where Grace is."

Laurie was speaking so fast that Echo did not have time to respond in his usual manner. "Going back into Carmella's room seems like my only option."

Laurie felt into the cleavage of her bra to be sure the key was still there, where she put it this morning on her way to the kitchen. "It looks like I'm on my own."

"On my own!" Echo squawked.

"It's what I must do …and quickly, before Carmella returns!"

Laurie can hear the others tidying up the kitchen while she sneaks down the hall to Carmella's room. The key is still warm from her breasts as she slides it into the lock and this time the door opens easily, without a creaking sound. As she slips back inside, she watches the hallway until the last possible moment for anyone who might be coming and then quietly closes the door.

The room looks nearly untouched. That is, except the bed seems a bit askew, the headboard pulled ever so slightly away from the wall. Laurie tip toes over, her heart pounding in her ears. There, tucked between the headboard and the wall is Carmella's satchel. Laurie decides she must be brave. She gives the satchel a tug to free it from the wedge and sets it on the bed.

Quickly, she unzips it and flips through the contents. Aside from a couple of legal documents at the very top of the stack, there is nothing too interesting. Then, she comes across Frankie's birth certificate…issued in Italy!

She methodically glances around the room….*the tea set is missing. That's odd, so is the cart.* She can feel the intensifying pressure of the timing on this discovery and her feeling that she must share the birth certificate with Irene as quickly as possible, before Carmella and Frankie return. She sets the certificate aside and gathers the other papers, dropping several in her haste.

Laurie stoops to retrieve the rogue documents and notices the ants have made it into this room as well. The trail crosses from a place next to the door, across the room just in front of the bed and down into the craggy crack beneath the mirror into the space between the floor and the wall.

"Damn Ants! They're everywhere!" she whispers, as she replaces the other papers and zips the satchel closed, tucking it back where she found it between the headboard and the wall.

It seems she cannot move fast enough now as she takes Frankie's Italian birth certificate, leaves the room and places the key on its nail behind the ominous gaze of the photo on the wall.

22 What's Love Got To Do With It?

Laurie is nearly breathless from the stress of her adventure and discovery. "Irene, look! I've found something really important in Carmella's room!"

Irene backs away, turning to leave. "Laurie, I thought we agreed you weren't going to go nosing around."

"I didn't agree to that." Laurie follows her into the living room. "The only thing on my mind was to try to find out what's going on around here and what has happened to Grace. I mean, nothing has been normal since she and I went into Carmella's room the other night. I had asked her to go back in with me once again, but she refused. And then, she disappeared. I thought just maybe…Please, I've found something really important, even if it doesn't help us figure out where Grace went!"

"Alright, show me what you've found. But just remember; if Carmella finds out; this was totally your doing!"

The pair has not noticed Etta, now standing in the doorway. "What's going on here?"

"You don't want to know," Irene answers.

"Laurie?" Etta demands.

"Ok...I went into Carmella's room...I found her satchel in there... behind the headboard of the bed. Oh, my God, my heart is pounding! I know you don't approve, but I am just desperate for answers about why Grace hasn't turned up. Look... it's Frankie's birth certificate - she was born in Italy!"

Irene takes the certificate from Laurie and studies it for a moment. "You are correct - I don't approve. And I cannot imagine how you think this might contribute to finding Grace. Now you've added yet another layer to this mystery. Seriously, an Italian certificate of birth for a child she's never, ever mentioned before? What on earth can this be about?"

"It's about that gangster she was married to, that's what!" Etta locks her wrists firmly on her hips.

Irene looks puzzled, "Gangster? And why are you calling him a gangster?"

"Because that's exactly how he behaved!" The expression on Etta's face reveals her distaste for the man.

"Wait, I'm confused!" Laurie questions, "What are we talking about?"

"Don't feel left out, Laurie, I'm as confused as you are," Irene whines. "Etta, are you talking about the man she loved to go dancing with when she was young?"

"Exactly," Etta explains, "the handsome, well-suited man in the old photographs - the one that got away."

"Why do you call him 'the one that got away'? I mean, you just said they were married, right?"

"Yes, married just long enough to break her heart. She once told me he's the reason she still dances to this day. She said she's never stopped dreaming of him; never stopped loving him."

"Wait just a minute, Etta. You and Carmella don't even like each other. This hurts. How is it you know so much about her husband?"

"We have history together."

"History?" Irene seems to be trying to grasp it all, "History? What does that mean?"

"I don't know why I should tell you two jaybirds any of this. But ok, you asked for it, and Carmella's definitely never been on my list of favorite people anyway. In fact, I'm not sure why I have kept all of this bottled up for so long. It certainly couldn't have and shouldn't have been out of respect for the woman. Maybe it was pity..."

Irene grows impatient, "Could you please get to the point?"

"Well, all right, I can't see any reason to keep her secrets quiet any longer. Do you remember when Grace said this isn't the first time that things just haven't added up where Carmella's concerned, and she mentioned a hit-and-run investigation?"

"Oh, yes...," Irene's thoughts deepen, "Now that you bring it up, I do remember."

Laurie is holding her head between her hands, "What? My thoughts are spinning! I am so confused! There isn't time for this! Grace is still missing!"

"Do you want to hear this, Laurie?" Etta asks. "Are you sure you can handle it?"

"I guess that depends on what IT is!"

Etta hesitates before continuing; "IT is the investigation the police conducted on Carmella and her husband, Nick, for a hit-and-run car accident she was involved in many, many years ago. They were actually investigating a more recent occurrence when they discovered references to an incident from many years earlier. The most recent incident was deemed a simple accident that Carmella was not held responsible for."

"But you see, the new investigation brought the earlier incident back into the light and after so many years the police finally learned that the injured woman from the earlier collision spent eighteen months in rehabilitation for her injuries; meanwhile Nick and Carmella had just gone on with their lives. The police wanted to know why the accident had never been fully investigated."

"And?" Irene asks.

"There is no 'and.' Most immediately the whole investigation was dropped. The injuries from the accident cost the victim the bulk of her career, and ultimately her marriage from all the stress, and nearly destroyed her life. Carmella was behind the wheel, but it was that man, Nick, who acted as if the whole affair was just another problem to be solved."

"I don't get it," Irene comments.

Etta continues, "The truth was that near the time the victim was to be released from her doctor's care, Nick paid her a friendly visit. He firmly insisted that where the police were concerned the victim should 'clam up,' and accept his offer to 'be taken care of for life; or consider not having one,' as he put it."

"Not having 'one' what?"

"A life," Etta frowns.

"Oh my God! I'm shocked to hear you say this!" Irene presses for more details, "Where did you get all of this? How could you possibly know if these things are true? On second thought, how could you even know these things? And who is this alleged hit and run victim?"

Etta pauses, and for a moment, the women are not sure she will answer. "It was me."

"What?!!!!" Both women exclaim in shock.

"It's true. That's how I ended up living here. That was the deal I made." Etta slowly shakes her head before continuing. "Dancing with the Devil, I guess you could say. Or, Devils in this case."

Laurie begins to understand, "Are you saying you are being taken care of by Carmella? Are you saying...?"

"It's true, I took Nick's threat seriously, and I 'clammed up'....now this 'bird' lives here rent free forever: An all-expenses-paid existence in return for my forever silence." Etta offers a remorseful chuckle, "It's a special kind of coop created especially for the chickens of this world – like me."

"Oh my God, Etta," Laurie tries to comfort her.

"What happened to Carmella's husband?" Irene asks.

"I don't know." Etta adds, "Except for that day when their car collided with me, I never saw them together as a couple again. Actually, I never actually saw him again after our little talk when I was recovering in the hospital."

"He actually visited you in the hospital?"

Etta chuckles to herself, "It wasn't a friendly visit, Laurie. He wanted only to keep himself and Carmella from 'further complications,' as he called it. The house was made ready for my release from the hospital and therapy. It was all set up and all I had to do was shut up and show up."

"I'm trying to accept the possibility that your story is all true," Irene says as she slumps onto the sofa, still holding the birth certificate. "My God. You've been living here ever since."

"Yes. So, there you have it. Do you still think you know her, Irene? Still think she's a wonderful friend?"

"I… I truly do not know what to think. Or to say…"

23 THE ONE -WAY TICKET

Laurie's stress is growing. "Girls, we have to focus on finding Grace!"

Unbeknownst to the women, Carmella has returned and overheard the last bit of their discussion through the open window. She bursts through the door.

"Saying nothing – keeping your mouth shut - is still the order of the day! Etta, you surprise me; we had an agreement!"

Etta stands her ground, "It's an agreement I've never felt good about. I'm tired, Carmella. I lost my way here at the Manor. I should have found the courage to leave long ago. I don't want to be involved in whatever this thing with Frankie is. And the vague unrest I've felt for years, it suddenly crystallized for me and I realized my life is never going to change, because I'm living in yours. You're controlling it all. You are 'the man behind the curtain' in my life - my own personal Wizard of Oz!"

"You ungrateful, little bitch!" Carmella pulls a small revolver from her shoulder bag and points it at Etta.

Irene starts to stand, but Carmella shoves her, almost playfully, back onto the sofa, "How about I kill you all?"

"Oh, come on!" Etta crows "Are you kidding? You'd kill us just because your secret's out?"

Laurie gasps, "Oh, my God!"

"Kill us?" Irene's words catch in her throat. "I can't believe my ears. Carmella, please - we're friends, I've loved you. I don't understand."

"Carmella!" Etta challenges, "Now you're acting like Nick! You learned that 'bravado' from him."

"Listen, Carmella," Irene tries to reason, "We can talk this out."

"Relax, Irene. You've been pining away, wanting to be with your poor, dead Barney for months now. Here's your chance."

"Carmella, please," Laurie interjects. She can see that the power surging forth inside Carmella is an attempt to intimidate them.

"Silence!"

"Stop, Carmella, please, you are scaring me," Irene pleads. "Please don't point the gun at me. I really don't want to be with Barney. I want to be here with my friends, like you."

"Shut up, Irene. Let's try not to complicate this with your imaginary friendship."

Irene presses on, "Imaginary friendship? It's real for me, Carmella. Please tell me, when were you in Italy? This certificate says Frankie was born to you in Florence. You've never said a word about being out of the country for the birth of a child."

"I never talk about it!" Carmella's face blushes with anger and shame. "Not ever! If you must know, being pregnant with Frankie cost me everything! I was crazy in love with Nick – everything about him; his deep olive colored skin, his silky black hair, his smile. And, oh…how we danced! His strong arms were my entire world. We were in love! He sent me a one-way ticket. He took me to his mother's home in Italy. And then the bastard abandoned me for New York when I unexpectedly became pregnant."

Irene begins to stand again, but Carmella, still pointing the pistol, motions her back into the chair.

Laurie and Etta seem frozen, unsure of what to do, as Irene keeps pressing Carmella for answers. Irene seems so small, huddling on the couch. She asks softly, "But, wouldn't his mother help you?"

"The women had no authority in that family, so No! I was on my own. He didn't want the baby or me. To make matters worse, my own family disowned me over the pregnancy."

"Then how…?"

"Shut up! No more. I have to think. I've come way too far to let you women unravel my life in front of this town."

No one notices as Etta slowly inches her way backward, away from Carmella and Irene, toward the fireplace. In one smooth move, she snatches the Golden Brick Award from the mantel, leaps onto the coffee table and hits Carmella from behind, squarely on the head!

Laurie scurries sideways as Carmella slowly crumples to the floor.

"Look, she's melting," Etta exclaims with a grin. "I've always wanted to do that!"

"And now," Irene declares, "I am the one who is calling the police. Carmella is some friend, indeed!"

24 FORTY-EIGHT HOURS

The police and the paramedics arrive in no time. As one of the officers handcuffs Carmella to the gurney, the others begin questioning Irene, Laurie, and Etta about the events of the day.

They might have handcuffed Etta too for using the Golden Brick Award as a weapon, except the handcuffs were hardly suited for her pudgy little wrists and short arms. Besides, the fact that she was an old woman, supposedly defending them all against a crazed person with a gun, caused the officers to reconsider, so they requested Etta remain seated on a chair instead.

It's Irene's turn to tell the story, and all she can keep saying is that she mistakenly thought she and Carmella were friends. "Friends for years," Etta interjects from her seat in the corner as she rolls her eyes.

The officer seems to be growing weary from trying to get 'just the facts' out of Irene, so at least he turns to look at Laurie when she interrupts to exclaim, "It's four o'clock."

"So? Don't interrupt," Irene demands. "The officer's interviewing ME about my shock of discovering my 'friend' wasn't a friend after all...I mean she did pull a gun on me!"

"Please," Laurie interrupts again, talking as fast as she can to get it all out. "I'm keeping track - it's been forty-eight hours since we realized that Grace has gone missing. You police wouldn't listen to me before. Can we please talk about it now? Last time I saw her she was wearing a plaid shirt and a red apron with a pocket full of Honey Seed crackers, and her birds are waiting. They are hungry and if we don't hurry; well I mean, the birds and Grace must really be in trouble - I'm sure of it. I know that maybe it's not logical, but I can just feel it!"

"You called the station a couple of days ago, right?" the Officer recalled. "Slow down. Tell me what you think has happened."

"It's not what I think, it's what I know! Grace would not have just left. Something is wrong! And she wouldn't have taken all the Honey Seed crackers with her - I couldn't find them where they usually are for feeding the birds!"

"There are no seed crackers, no note and no Grace!"

Silently, as if in slow motion, thousands of dead ants begin falling from the rafters above them.

"Oh, my God!" Laurie screams as the hardened bodies pile up on the officer's hat and shoulders and in Laurie's hair as she tries to deal with the horror of it all! "It's raining dead ants! Just like the Bug Woman said it would!"

Suddenly Laurie stops struggling and holds out her hands, palms up, watching the ants bounce off her skin.

"Ants - That's it! Honey Seed crackers! I remember seeing ants by the crack in the wall in Carmella's room. Ants follow honey! Grace must have gone back in! Now that's solid, logical thinking! Come on - follow me: I think Grace is somewhere in Carmella's secret room and the ants followed her there!"

Laurie quickly retrieves the key from behind the picture and unlocks the door of Carmella's private room. The ant trail is as active as ever, crossing the room just as she had recalled and going down through the craggy crack, just below the mirror, between the plaster wall and the wooden floor.

The commotion caused by the three women and the officer's boots upon the floor planks rouses Grace from her stupor. Still too sore for much movement, she struggles to throw the dead batteries and the flashlight and anything loose she can find nearby toward the staircase.

Carefully avoiding the spot where the bone was, she makes as much noise as possible and calls out to them.

"Down here! I'm here!"

Moments seem like forever, but the mirror is pushed aside revealing the stairwell, and Grace can see her rescuers silhouetted in the light from above as they descend into the cellar.

The officers' flashlights illuminate the area of the wall where Grace has propped herself. "Look, I'm not certain it was Carmella, but someone shoved the tea cart down the steps, just as I was coming up. I'm pretty sure my arm is broken, and my back hurts so much from the fall that I have trouble standing and certainly can't walk on my own."

The officer's move the tea cart and start to work their way through the broken cups and tea set. "We'll get you out, just hold on another moment."

"Watch out for the bones – don't step there!" she exclaims.

"Bones?"

"Yes, shine your light there," she points to the femur. "That's human, right?"

"Yes, I'd say so," the officer agrees as he turns to the doorway at the top of the stairs where the other women wait.

"Ladies, I have to ask you to leave the room…and don't touch a thing." He adds, "This room is now off limits while we investigate! We will be taping it off - it is officially a crime scene."

Laurie wishes she could hug Grace while she watches two newly arrived paramedics work on Grace while the others from the first ambulance finish checking the bump on Carmella's head in the other room.

The police prepare to take Carmella away. She hides her face from the people who have gathered on the street. And although she had asked the officers not to use the siren, they seem to enjoy the fact that the police car's flashing lights and the ambulance's siren are enough to cause some obvious discomfort in Carmella as they drive away, ever so slowly through the neighborhood.

25 SOME REALLY CRAZY STORY

Hidden within the crowd on the sidewalk, Frankie is staying just far enough back to be sure she will not be noticed. After the police car carrying Carmella leaves and the ambulance pulls away with Grace on board, Frankie approaches the home. She knocks softly.

When Irene opens the door of Carmella Manor, Frankie speaks quickly, just in case the women do not welcome her presence, "I'm not sure what's gone on here, but at least I can see that my mother isn't inside. I just stopped by to say goodbye. I'm going back to California. Look, I know there has been some trouble here. And I know you wouldn't think I'd care, but I am hoping that it didn't have anything to do with me coming here."

"It didn't, not directly anyway," Irene answers.

"Why did the police take my mother? What did she do?"

"They are holding her for questioning," Irene explains. "Luckily we found Grace, and aside from a broken arm, she should be okay."

"Found Grace?"

Etta steps up, "Carmella locked Grace in the cellar."

Frankie shakes her head, "Well, I'd like to say I am shocked, but I am not. Shoving the truth and her troubles somewhere dark is just her style. Sorry to hear it. Listen, it's time I was on my way. Thanks again for your kindness and the bit of help you had offered."

"No problem," Irene answers.

Frankie adds with a laugh, "Well, at least for once it looks like I wasn't the biggest problem going on!"

As she turns to leave, Frankie notices the baby photo and the little shoes on the coffee table. "Would you mind if I took these?"

The women are startled at her request, realizing she obviously knows something that might help solve the mystery.

"Why? Do you know who the baby boy is?" they ask, practically in unison.

Frankie holds back a giggle, "It's not a boy, it's me."

"You! Oh, thank God!" Laurie exclaims, "Then you're not buried underneath the house!"

Frankie looks baffled, "What?"

"Never mind," Irene quips. "Laurie, you're an idiot!" Irene points to the baby in the photo, "Frankie,

THAT'S you? Why were you dressed like a boy, all in blue?"

"Some really crazy story my mother told me! She said my father didn't really want a baby and wouldn't help her, unless she had a son. She said she had pleaded with him - she desperately wanted to get back to the U.S."

She smiles down at the photo in her hand, "You gotta give her points for guts! She told me that when I was born a girl, she didn't give up. Would you expect her to? I wouldn't - not me. Nope"

Laurie takes the photo from her, wanting a closer look. "I don't understand..."

"Well, you will; It was a simple plan, but, as I think of it now, really clever. My mother said she named me Francesca, called me 'Frankie' for short just to confuse Nick, dressed me all in blue and had a photo taken to send to him...the thug."

"Oh, now I get it!" Laurie grins, "And it worked? He sent her the tickets?"

"Evidently. But she said he was furious when they reunited and he discovered she had lied!"

Frankie twirls the baby shoes around by the laces, "Serves him right!"

26 MATTERS OF THE HEART

Laurie has been doing her best to keep the animals fed the past few days while Grace has been away, recuperating from her fall.

Now, Grace has returned and announced she has decided to leave Carmella estate. Her suitcase is filled and the Peace Roses are packed onto the house trailer for travel. Still wearing a cast on her arm, Grace has had to take some extra time tidying things and she is nearly finished closing up the workshed.

The women have gathered to say goodbye, and together they marvel at how different Grace seems since the accident and her soul-searching time alone in the cellar.

"I can't believe she is leaving us," Laurie comments. "And I can't decide if it is a good thing, or a bad thing; I mean where she is concerned."

"Well," Josephine comments, "that wouldn't be for you to decide; it's all up to her."

Locking the door of the workshed for the last time, Grace walks slowly through the green grass, nearly like always. However, today Grace is wearing a beautiful lavender dress and low-heeled, creamy patent leather shoes instead of her usual gardening attire.

"I can't ever remember seeing her look so nice," Josephine comments. "Don't you all agree?"

"Yes, she certainly seems different since the ordeal." Laurie, Etta, and Irene watch as Grace pauses to smell the garden's roses she has tended for all these many years gone by.

"I can see that somehow it all helped her, even though it was really bad at the time. She said the experience is what made her realize it is time to move on. In fact, her experience opened my eyes too," Etta comments.

"Well, as strange as it is to admit, it had an effect on me too," Irene adds. "I suddenly realized that life is short. Barney is gone, but I'm still here, and it's not too late. I need to decide what happens next for me."

Grace beams with happiness as she picks a flower and crosses lawn. Josephine is smiling, her eyes fixed on Grace as she draws nearer. "She seems more 'colorful' somehow…a different sort of a bird now."

Laurie adds, "Yeah, a peacock!"

"It's true, Grace seems to have truly spread her wings and become something more complete, more beautiful than she was," Josephine smiles.

"That's it," Grace tells them. "I've set the last of the healthy birds free and they've flown off into the morning sky," she smiles as she joins the women.

"Oh, Grace," Laurie exclaims. "How exciting! Now what will you do, where will you go?"

"No place in particular, maybe everywhere," she replies. "All I know is that I've spent a lifetime saving others, and when it came down to what I thought might be my last hours, I realized I'd never saved myself. So, that's where I'm going! Home to myself!"

Laurie sweeps Grace into a big hug.

Grace seems taken by surprise, ""Wow! What's with you, Laurie?"

"I just need to thank you," she answers.

"Thank ME? It was you and your persistent nature that helped get me out of that horrible cellar!"

Grace hugs her in again. "So, thank YOU! I tell you, the pain was severe, and I don't think I could have survived another day on just the dirty rainwater leaking in and Honey Seed crackers! Still I am grateful beyond words for living through it and being able to go back to my life."

Laurie is fighting back tears, "Grace, it's just that you have taught me so much. Whether you realize it or not, you are my hero! Because of your example through the years, when it really mattered, when I had to depend only on myself to figure out what happened to you, something miraculous happened; I trusted my MIND! And I suddenly trusted myself – I trusted my own instincts! I feel I owe this, in part, to you, Grace!"

"Oh, Laurie, you seem so much stronger! This is truly great news!"

"I realized I couldn't take the pressure and stress of figuring things out logically, the way I had been taught to approach everything! I just knew you were in trouble and I was sure I could find you! So, I gave up on the logical approach - it just wasn't working. I suddenly knew how to listen to my own woman's intuition! In fact, even when no one else was listening to me, I could hear myself figuring it out! It began when I asked myself, 'What would Grace do?' Now I'm able to ask myself, 'What should I do?' And then I find my way!"

"Well you'll certainly fly high with that!" Grace smiles lovingly at Laurie. "Listen, I haven't really spoken to any of you about everything that happened-I'm just curious, what's to become of Carmella?"

"Same here," adds Josephine. "I missed most of the excitement. Catch me up…"

"The police are still holding her while they investigate what happened here at Carmella Manor. Not only what happened here just recently, but other things as well," Irene explains.

Etta adds, "Grace, make sure you stay in touch so we can keep you filled in on the details. Of course the investigators will most likely need to speak with you, especially about the bone."

"What 'other things' are you referring to?"

"Well, it is bad enough she's being charged with kidnapping and assault over what she did to you," Irene comments. "But…no one's told you yet? The mystery of that bone in the basement may have been solved."

Grace shudders, "I think finding the bone was the worst of it. No, as I said, I'm a little out of touch. So, what's the story?"

"Well, Irene's 'friend' Carmella is being held for possible murder charges!" Etta adds, "Can you believe it? The police found more bones and are investigating the high probability that they are the remains of Carmella's husband...you know, the photo in the hall, that guy. Turns out he hasn't been seen for years. With his underworld ties, nobody dared look into it...until now."

"Holy Purple Cow!" Josephine pats Grace on the shoulder. "I wouldn't have imagined all of this about Carmella."

Grace's attention drifts as she enjoys her last looks at the changing light in the garden she so loved. She is barely listening as Etta tries to go on with everything she had kept secret for years upon years.

"Knowing now that Nick might be dead, and Carmella is in jail has suddenly, I realized, set me free!"

The secrets tumbled from Etta's lips:

"Carmella really had a tumultuous past: She met Nick in Italy. She loved to dance and she always said he wooed her with a sexy tango on a moonlit night. They married most immediately, but then he abandoned her."

Etta continues, "It was always so strange to hear her speak of him; she idolized him and could never really get past his betrayal."

A frown crosses Etta's face as she goes on, "I hated him for the deal we had made: I might as well have been their prisoner here in Carmella Manor. I mean, what else was I going to do, but stay? And hour upon hour she would speak of her love for him."

"You know," Irene interjects, "I do remember now that she once told me it was those first happy memories of him which have kept her dancing to this day."

Etta adds, "Yes, she can dance circles around any twenty-year-old! Every chance she gets, she puts on her little heels and goes to the clubhouse to dance, to hold a stranger in her arms and dream of Nick."

"Heels?" Josephine looks down at her own heavy, broken down ankles. "I couldn't get into a pair of high heel shoes to save my soul, let alone go dancing in them! How can a brittle woman her age dance in heels?"

"I'm proud to say I know the answer to this. It's simple: she put them on when he came into her life and she's never quit wearing them, and she's never stopped dancing!"

"Well," Laurie offers, "she may be a good dancer, but evidently her intuitions aren't so good...I mean if he really had connections to the mob!"

"And," Etta adds, "clearly her love for him kept her stuck in memories from the past."

"I went to see her at the jail," Irene confesses. "She suddenly looks old and frail."

"Well, I have to admit, I'm not feeling much sympathy for the woman. I'm just grateful to have survived and to have the chance to move on...into a better life," Grace smiles.

"Survival!" Laurie exclaims, "There's that word again! Seems like survival plays a big part in all of our lives! Wouldn't you say so?"

"I hear you," says Grace.

"Amen" adds Irene.

"Survival instinct is what leads us along - it's how we find our way," exclaims Etta. "In fact, I'd say survival is The Yellow Brick Road!"

"You, of all people, would say that!" Irene laughs.

They all chuckle and Irene adds, "Yes, looks like it might always be about survival. When I visited the jail, Carmella finally shared a bit of her own secret of survival with me. You know, turns out we really are friends after all."

She continues, "And in an ironic sort of way, if you ignore the details, we both kept ourselves in cages we built around our lives. Cages constructed from our youthful, girlish ideas about what it means to love a man. I can't believe how much time was lost."

She adds, "At least I have a chance to see things differently, and to change the way I will go on without Barney. Carmella's not so fortunate."

She continues, "The way she tells it, when her husband discovered the child was a girl, a big argument ensued over her deception. He threatened to bury Carmella in the basement, and then he tried to kill her with his bare hands while the baby slept in a cradle nearby," Irene explains.

"Luckily," she continues, "Carmella says that at the last moment he lost his footing and fell down the stairs into the cellar. As he lay unconscious from the fall, Carmella shot him on the spot with his own gun. She told me she used a toy sandbox shovel to bury him right where he fell and has guarded the secrets of her past ever since."

"Wow, I knew she was crazy!" Josephine exclaims, "Now I can see why! That's a lot to keep bottled up inside! I always felt she was hiding something big. But this is incredible! That kind of explains why she didn't want to live here."

"You know, I think I actually have the heart to forgive her," Irene comments. "That secret and deciding what to do about raising a rebellious daughter like Frankie had to be a horrible burden to shoulder all alone."

"She did have some hefty secrets," Etta adds. "But even knowing the things I knew, this is way more drama than I could have ever imagined!" She pauses, deep in a thought.

"I guess I can't put all the blame on her for the way I have lived ever since the accident. Irene, what you said about the emotional cage you built hit a nerve with me. Damn, I can see now how I willingly participated in this whole thing; how I bought into the fear and the threats…do you think that makes me an accomplice?"

Grace chuckles, "Not if you didn't know about the murder!"

As Grace starts to lift her suitcase, Irene is quick to give her an unexpected hand. "Please, let me get that for you."

Laurie grows tearful, "I hate goodbyes! Oh, Grace! I wish you would stay. I hate to think of you out there all alone."

"Never said I was going alone," Grace's smile widens. "Amelia and I have decided to have a go at a little 'free flight'!"

"Amelia...The exterminator?" they all ask in unison.

"It's Amelia the Bug Woman! She has made a fortune with her business over the years, relieving people of their pests. It turns out that in an odd way, we're both alike...Seems she is as tired of killing things as I am of saving things! We're thinking maybe we'll balance each other out!"

As they all enjoy a good laugh together Josephine tosses a playful thought into the mix, "Hey, Grace, maybe like a fancy affair, you should have held back releasing the animals and queued the release of a dozen birds as you and Amelia ride off into the sunset with your trailer full of Peace Roses!"

She adds, "Oh, and sweetheart, I've been meaning to ask; did you lose any birds while you were trapped in the cellar?"

"A few," Grace replies. "I tell you, being trapped in the cellar, and knowing now I that I was in there with a dead man's bones is one experience which truly changed my life. And it made me realize that in spite of all I've ever done for every one of the creatures, the sick, weak ones just didn't make it. They didn't survive."

Hugging together, sharing their tears, Grace continues, "You know, in many ways I've always thought of us girls as 'wounded birds,' but now I've realized how strong we really are! The birds that did survive stayed strong - they'll be fine. And so will we!"

ABOUT LYNN ALISON TROMBETTA

Lynn Alison Trombetta is an American author whose whimsical adult fiction plays with the edges of reality. She writes to reconnect with the magic of true spirit for a joyful, limitless life based personal creative evolution and awareness.

Wounded Birds is her second novella.

Lynn Alison is also a visual artist and professional flutist in the group *Meadowlark*. She resides in Sedona, Arizona with her husband and performing partner, guitarist Rick Cyge.

Friend her at facebook.com/lynntrombettawriter and visit her website to sign up for her mailing list at www.LynnTrombetta.com.

OTHER PUBLICATIONS
by Lynn Alison Trombetta

Pie in the Skye, a novella…A fantastic journey through the landscape of your imagination into the knowing of your heart.

Meadowlark CDs and Digital Music:

First Light ; Celtic and original music

Legend of the Land ; Visually Evocative originals

FreeFall ; Joyful, celebratory original music

Tranquility ; Relaxing original music for inspiration, contemplation and massage.

Visit Lynn Trombetta.com